Susan Hunt

SEASONS OF LOVE

Limited Special Edition. No. 18 of 25 Paperbacks

Susan is fortunate enough to live between two riverside properties, one on the banks of the River Lune in Lancashire, the other on Bodmin Moor beside the River Inny, a few miles from the rugged north Cornish coast, providing much of the inspiration for her debut novel.

Susan attributes her sense of fun to having spent her entire adult life in the company of young children. If not in the workplace, then as Brown Owl or Sunday School teacher in a village hall. But, first and foremost, as a mother to her four children and three grandchildren.

For my youngest son, Billy, yet to discover that love and passion really do exist in later life. X

Susan Hunt

SEASONS OF LOVE

God Bless

Susan Hunt.

AUSTIN MACAULEY PUBLISHERS™
LONDON • CAMBRIDGE • NEW YORK • SHARJAH

Copyright © Susan Hunt (2019)

The right of Susan Hunt to be identified as author of this work has been asserted by her in accordance with section 77 and 78 of the Copyright, Designs and Patents Act 1988.

All rights reserved. No part of this publication may be reproduced, stored in a retrieval system, or transmitted in any form or by any means, electronic, mechanical, photocopying, recording, or otherwise, without the prior permission of the publishers.

Any person who commits any unauthorised act in relation to this publication may be liable to criminal prosecution and civil claims for damages.

A CIP catalogue record for this title is available from the British Library.

ISBN 9781788787871 (Paperback)
ISBN 9781528956116 (ePub e-book)

www.austinmacauley.com

First Published (2019)
Austin Macauley Publishers Ltd
25 Canada Square
Canary Wharf
London
E14 5LQ

Thank you to Martin for your valuable support.
Thanks also to all at Austin Macauley involved in the publication of my first novel.

All the characters and events in this publication, other than those clearly in the public domain, are fictitious and any resemblance to real persons, living or dead, is purely coincidental.

Prologue
Summer 2010

It had been mid-afternoon when Molly and Frank had arrived at the holiday cottage they'd rented for a couple of weeks for the second time this year, eager to return and explore what was now beginning to feel like home.

On their last day, as they were driving back to pack, they had noticed a "For Sale" board being driven into the front garden of a beautiful white-washed cottage, above the village in which they were staying. It was then that they had decided to set about making their dream come true.

Exactly one year later, the removal van had pulled up outside Honeysuckle cottage, the very same cottage that had made them realise their dream.

Chapter 1
October 2015
Down Memory Lane

I wake from my slumber, as I jump back into Wednesday afternoon. I had been enjoying the comfort and warmth of a cup of tea in the afternoon sun in a strategically placed armchair in the kitchen, to which I'm an avid visitor at this time of year. I had mown the lawn for probably the last time this year, although it won't be long before the leaves start to litter the green carpet. There is already a scattering of large, lovely red leaves on the sun-drenched path. Despite it being cosy sitting here, there is quite a breeze outside, creating a nip in the air. The tall trees at the bottom of the garden are restless, as though fighting the inevitable. The cat soon returned once the mower had been put away, finding herself a warm spot in the sunshine to sleep some more.

The garden has changed a little since you saw it last; the trees are still mostly green, although some remind me of dinner, browning and bubbling under the grill, in stark contrast to the bright pansies which look good enough to eat! The fruit from the garden has all been eaten, apart from the falling baking apples I pick up regularly, which must mean its blackberry picking season. The birds have all flown their nests from inside the hedge and no longer visit. The geraniums, appearing blissfully unaware of the onset of frost; I will have to bring them in if I am to enjoy them again.

Realising the time, my thoughts quickly return to my plans for the afternoon, including calling at the florist before seeing you. I almost run up the stairs to grab my coat, which I find still hanging in the wardrobe after not being worn for many months. It smells warm and comforting and embraces me like an old friend, making the onset of winter a little less daunting. You chose the coat for me when we first moved here, so I wouldn't look out of place in my long-tailored wool coat from the city. I hurry down the stairs again, picking up the post from the floor, which can be opened when I return. I collect my keys and the book I share with you, slipping it deep into a pocket. As soon as I open the door I'm hit by the passing breeze; autumn has definitely arrived! The coat, a heavy tartan-lined waxed jacket, was certainly a good idea. I pull up the collar and dig my hands into the pockets, pulling out a piece of paper which I unfold curiously, then dismiss, stuffing it back into the depths, where it has lain undisturbed for so long.

I begin the familiar route down into the village, passing rows of cottages cramming the hillside for the best views. I soon pass the pink cottage on the corner, the colour of marshmallows. Today there are eggs for sale! I remember stopping to buy some strawberries with you one day on our way home for lunch, devouring most of them before we'd reached our garden gate! I continue on past the holiday cottages, which all appear empty and quiet, no vehicles on their driveways with adornments on their roof bars, although it won't be long before we see their return for a short spell, unlike the swallows, who won't be back until spring.

It must be home time as I can hear the school children in the distance, before a Land Rover filled with small children squeezes past me, releasing the honeysuckle fragrance from the hedgerow. I notice the blackberries glowing in the sunlight and can't resist popping one in my mouth—soft, warm and sweet, ripe for the picking, knowing if you were here you would return with a bowl, picking enough for me to bake a crumble to eat with vanilla ice cream. I can taste it now!

I turn right at the Smugglers Inn, which appears dark and quiet. A different story come evening, its little square windows aglow, and the smell of the huge log fire, warm and welcoming, but never the less quiet. A cyclist passes me and is soon out of sight. The road is quiet, apart from the usual parents on their familiar route home from school; many of whom went to the school themselves, as did their parents. We are lucky to still have a local school; many are closed now, having become private residences, or even restaurants. I stuff my hands into my pockets to warm them from the chill, and feeling the folded paper I'd discovered earlier, open it up to reveal the carol service from last year, nearly a year ago now. Unfolding it is like opening the church door, releasing gold, frankincense and myrrh. My thoughts change as I approach the shops, and even before turning into the narrow winding street I can smell the fresh fish, all caught locally and presented behind a large picture window, on display like some fine art. There are two women sitting in the tea shop next door, chatting over a pot of steaming hot tea. Not so long ago there would have been a steady flow of families choosing ice creams from the extensive range on offer throughout the summer months; a palate of colour and flavour to refresh and tempt the tourists.

Across the street is Dan's studio and gallery, displaying familiar scenes from local artists, including a painting of yours. The window is beautifully lit to draw attention to the magnificent work on display. The street is mainly made up of cottages, interspersed with the occasional shop or establishment the community might need. As well as the pub up the road, there is a little bar-restaurant that takes advantage of the views beyond with its outside terrace, also boasting a fine dining experience—more oysters and Champagne than the pie and a pint served up the road. 'Kelvins' also offers a couple of en suite rooms and provides work for local students during the summer months, as does the tea shop up the road. Even the little school children take advantage of the influx of tourists, selling bags of shells they have collected from the local shores. The bakery is next with its distinct heart-warming smell drawing you inside. In the morning, the window is laden with fresh loaves of every shape and size and delicious cakes, pastries and pasties.

As I continue further down the steep and narrowing street and the daylight fades, lights start to appear in windows and smoke rises from the chimney pots of the cosy little cottages, one of the many things that attracted us here. Despite being autumn, there is still a colourful array of flowers outside Lyndsey's shop. There are pumpkins of every size, and several buckets of seasonal flowers. I wander into the crammed interior, whereupon I'm greeted by Lyndsey, who lives with Dan over the street, above the gallery. As well as flowers, she sells fresh locally grown fruit and vegetables, supplying the local restaurants. I am drawn to the vibrant heads of the dahlias, which I remember reminded you of your granddad's garden. Each one different, but beautiful. I eventually choose a mixed bunch, including one that reminds me of raspberry ripple ice cream, and another that looks like a giant dandelion!

'Are they for Frank?' Lyndsey asks, before wrapping them.

'Yes, I'm just on my way to see him,' I explain, before she bids me farewell and I step back out into the cold.

On the corner is the Post Office, which sells almost everything you could ever need or imagine, from groceries to buckets and spades. Facing me at the bottom of the street is the chemist and the village hall, which is used for all manner of things, including parties, the mother and toddler group, brass band practice on a Friday night, and next week the harvest supper! You have even been known to show your artwork there, even selling some during the summer months, when the tourists have had time to stop and admire the beauty of our coastline that you were able to capture, that they had fallen in love with and wanted to take home. Once again, I'm reminded how lucky we are to call here home. There is a poster on the door advertising the annual bonfire celebrations, which is always a magnificent explosion of colourful stars falling like leaves from the sky.

The village is behind me now, as the road continues with occasional clusters of cottages, all warm and welcoming. Then, beautiful hedgerows and farmland, an abundance of beauty, manifesting itself before me. Tom approaches me with his faithful companion by his side, returning from an afternoon stroll on the beach; we nod, and he mumbles, passing comment on the tide, before continuing on his way.

I open the creaky metal gate at the end of the path, shutting it gently, so as not to disturb the peace. I make my way to where you lie, and weary now, sit down beside you. I listen to the birds beyond the dunes, riding the breeze over the waves. I unwrap the flowers, their scent filling the air with your memories. I take out the book from my pocket to continue reading the last few pages that are left. The sun is setting now; the colours looking like they have been spilt across the sky, before they disappear into darkness.

I whisper 'God bless' before creeping silently away, closing the gate gently behind me.

Chapter 2
The Harvest Moon

I wake to a beautiful morning, the sun already creeping in around the curtains. Summer is over, and the farmers have once again gathered in their crops; a whole year has been and gone without you. I had wished on every star in the moonlit sky, and pleaded with God not to take you, but as the high tide arrived, it swept you away, along with the birds and butterflies, and the fields became bare once more. The skies had seemed to mourn your departure, until, a week later, when the sun shone, and the birds began to sing, as we arrived at the church to celebrate your life.

I wander down into the village to the bakery, to collect a fresh white, warm, crusty loaf for my lunch, but as there's a queue, I continue on down to the post office, with a birthday card and present for one of my god-daughters, Tilly (Mathilda) Grace: a pretty flask for her to take into the garden. Tilly will be nineteen on Saturday and I have known her since she was born, looking after both her and her older siblings in my role as a nanny. Tilly had always had an interest in gardening, from an early age she would design a garden on a plate, using whatever she could find from the beautiful garden surrounding the house that she grew up in, that was cared for by Tom, also employed by the Richardson family. Tilly was always happiest following Tom, who was keen to share all he knew.

Whilst waiting to be served, I happen to glance at the notice board beside me; I'm drawn to a blue card, a family seeking a nanny for two young children. Unfamiliar with the address, I ask Hugh behind the counter.

'Old Joe's place, the last lot of cottages before the churchyard. The family are new here, after a nanny,' he says.

I make a note of the contact number and send Tilly's card and present on their way. I begin my assent back up the hill; the warm sun seems to have attracted people out, meandering across the street. There's yet another explosive array of colour outside Lyndsey's shop: pumpkins, gourds, berries and dahlias, all beckoning your attention across from an equally bold print adorning Dan's window. I arrive outside the bakery, the warm smell drifting out through the open door.

Sally greets me, 'Hi Molly, I was hoping to catch you. See if you can help us out again this year with the Christmas cakes?'

'Of course, I'd love to. I suppose I'd better get shopping,' I say. The quantities, astronomical: nearly nine Kilograms of dried fruit, forty large eggs and two bottles of brandy are just some of the ingredients!

I was first asked to help bake Christmas cakes after admiring Sally's selection, disclosing I had always made my own and often more besides for friends and family. Sally had then asked if I could help them to achieve their demand, making another fifteen to sell.

The lady behind me joins in our conversation, asking if she needs to order a cake, explaining she won't have time to make one herself, preferring to buy one homemade in the village, rather than one from the supermarket.

Sally takes her name and phone number. It's then that I realise it's the same person who had put up the card up in the Post office. I explain the coincidence to her and, outside the shop, we talk for a while, Sarah explaining she hasn't lived here long and is eager to find a nanny as soon as possible, having accepted a position at the school to start after Christmas. Her father, who lives locally, has offered to look after Luke and Lizzie, her two young children, until someone suitable is found to take on the role. Without thinking it through, I tell her I may be able to help her out, explaining I was once a nanny myself, and although I wasn't looking for work, it might actually be a good idea. Sarah appears thrilled, inviting me back with her immediately to meet her two young children. I explain I am on my way home to decorate and deliver some gingerbread men, agreeing to meet later in the day.

As always, I have made too many biscuits, just in case one or two have burnt fingers or toes, enabling me to put some in a smaller tin to take to Sarah's. I tie each tin in red gingham ribbon and head out, calling first next door with a small present and card, along with the tin for Megan's sixth birthday party later this afternoon, when she arrives home from school. Lucy is outside when I open the door, tying balloons and bunting around the garden.

'Oh thank you Molly, the children will love them! Call in later if you like, Megan would love to see you,' she says.

'Thanks, I may do. I'll see what time it is when I get back,' I reply, before heading down to Sarah's. The thought of working with little children again fills me with joy, suddenly realising how much I have missed it; already planning all the things we could do together: fishing in rock pools, picnics on the beach, the list is endless!

Before I know it, I have arrived at Mistletoe Cottage. As I knock on the door, I can hear two excited little voices alerting their mother of my arrival. Sarah opens the door into a bright hallway, with Lizzie snuggled close to her. Beside her is Luke, whose eyes fix upon the tin. I'm invited into a large living room, choosing to sit on a beautiful floral sofa beside a large inglenook fireplace. Despite all the toys on the floor, Luke's gaze is transfixed on the tin, which I invite him to open to satisfy his curiosity. He appears thrilled, asking politely if he can have one.

'Me too!' squeals Lizzie.

Luke begins his interrogation, asking me all manner of things, including my knowledge on breeds of cows, the models of tractors and the history of Toy Story, which have all now been restored, and something I am adamant about: my favourite flavour of ice cream—dark chocolate, always! Once Luke is satisfied, Sarah, Lizzie and I move into the kitchen, leaving Luke to play with his toy farm. Lizzie amuses herself with her own toys whilst Sarah invites me to sit down at the dining room table, where we enjoy a pot of tea and a gingerbread man, sharing our stories that had brought us here. Although Sarah had only moved here in the last few months, she already knew most of the locals and the surrounding area as she had grown up here, moving away to go to university where she had met Henry, her husband. Since having children, they had wanted to make their home here, to be able to spend more time with her family: her father and brother, still both living in the family home she grew up in, and the family home for several generations. Sam, Sarah's brother, now living there with his girlfriend Kate.

'Kate owns a quaint little tea shop in the town, called "Kate's Cakes". Have you been there?' asks Sarah.

'No,' I reply.

'Oh, in which case, I will definitely have to take you. She makes the most delicious cream tea, and serves warm, gooey brownies with clotted cream. She serves everything on beautiful mismatched china that she's accumulated over the years, from either charity shops, jumble sales, or her dearly departed grandmother. The walls are lined with books,' she continues to explain. 'When she moved in with Sam, she hadn't known what to do with all the books she had accumulated and read herself, so, as the premises had previously been a book shop, she decided to keep it alive. Customers often bring in their old books, and it has grown from there,' says Sarah. 'You'd love it!'

Suddenly realising the time, Sarah explains the children will soon want their tea. So, we exchange numbers and say our goodbyes, and to Luke's relief, I leave the tin of gingerbread men, realising I would never be able to visit empty handed again!

Chapter 3
Handbags and Glad Rags

The following morning Sarah calls, inviting me to the harvest supper and dance on Friday night. Today is Tuesday! Sarah explains it will be a good opportunity to meet the rest of the family. How could I refuse! More interrogation! Once I put down the phone, I begin wondering what I could wear to such an event. I run upstairs and open my wardrobe; according to a recent study, it's said that an average woman will spend almost a year standing in front of her wardrobe door deciding what to wear! So, not having much time, I grab my keys and purse—a designer purse, bigger than your average, but smaller than a bag—given as a gift from Tilly's mother when I'd left. A gift I never thought I would use, but has, in fact, gone with everything, and everywhere I go; just the right size for my cards, keys and phone, and if I ever need a bigger bag, I just slip it inside. How ingenious!

    I know exactly where I'm heading, although it has been a long time since I have had to buy something new for an occasion. Thirty minutes later I arrive outside the designer shop I have only ever read about in a magazine in a hotel lounge. The window is beautiful, like a cake shop window enticing you inside, depicting exactly what I am hoping to achieve. I already have a pair of jeans and heals, so choose a couple of blouses to try on; each different, but both suitable for such an occasion. Unable to choose between the two, I decide to take them both and decide later. I enjoy the walk back to the car, pleased with my purchases and feeling quite special carrying them in the designer bag, completely forgetting the feeling of trepidation I had initially felt about the whole occasion. I can't understand why, but I actually feel more confident wearing new clothes, rather than something old and familiar! The rhyme 'Something old, something new' springs to mind. New offering optimism for the future, quite appropriate I suppose, though I won't be slipping a silver sixpence in my shoe!

***

Remembering to pick up the tin of white chocolate cookies I'd made earlier, along with my favourite purse that completes my outfit, making me feel very chic, I open the door and step out into the warm evening; in a couple of weeks the days will become shorter, the sun will rise earlier, and the garden will go to sleep.

I arrive outside Sarah's front door with time to spare and compose myself, despite having deliberated over which blouse to wear!

Sarah opens the door and invites me into the kitchen, whereupon she introduces everyone.

'This is Henry, my adorable husband!' Sarah announces, grabbing hold of his hand, beckoning her father from the other side of the room, 'Dad, come and meet Molly.'

'Jim,' he says, offering his hand to greet me; in his other hand is a bottle of Champagne he has brought with him. He is a tall, well presented gentleman, with broad shoulders and a warm smile, that reminds me of Luke.

'Would you care to join us in a glass of our harvest cocktail? It's something we do every year.' He continues, 'Champagne and sloe gin. It's a family tradition to celebrate the harvesting of the fruit. This is last year's vintage; it's said to improve with age.'

'Yes please, it sounds delicious!' I answer.

Sarah comes back in the room with Luke, dressed in his pyjamas and his wild hair tamed, followed by Sam, whom she introduces as her taller, younger brother.

Jim enquires if the cocktail meets with my approval, explaining how it's Sarah's job to prepare the berries and remember to turn the bottles.

In the middle of the island, in the centre of the room, is a plate of prepared oysters sitting on a bed of ice, alongside a pile of white linen serviettes.

'Help yourself,' Jim says, as the others begin taking them. Perhaps the fact they feature on the menu of all good restaurants around here, it's assumed I know what to do when presented with this delicacy. Fortunately, I had acquired this skill and knew exactly how to enjoy one.

'Ah, here's Kate,' Sarah announces, as a small girl, with her long black hair plaited down her back, walks into the room.

'Hello, you must be Molly,' she says, smiling. 'I've left Lizzie, she's nearly asleep. I'll take Luke up when you leave,' she tells Sarah, as she is handed a drink.

'Well, I'm off now to get set-up,' Sam says, slipping an oyster in his mouth, before kissing Kate goodbye.

It isn't long before we all follow Sam up the street, leaving Kate to put Luke to bed. Sarah chats away excitedly, saying how much she has been looking forward to the evening, unable to remember attending such an event since she was about eighteen.

Jim sighs. 'How much has changed since then.'

It isn't long before we all arrive at the village hall, festooned with fairy lights. We can hear Sam on his guitar, his mate Guy on his fiddle, and someone else on the accordion. The band rehearse whilst everyone finds their seats in the other room. Each table responsible for bringing their own drinks. Henry had already brought enough cider for us all, possibly the entire party! Having hidden it under our table, leaving barely enough room for anyone's feet. At least we won't go thirsty! We are all served a bouillabaisse: a local speciality, which is as good as ever, as are the portions! For the vegetarians amongst us, there is a hearty vegetable stew; then for dessert: apple pie with a generous dollop of thick cream.

'I wonder if the apples in the pie have come from the same orchard as the cider,' comments Henry.

'Not sure Sam would have considered their origin!' Sarah laughs.

'He made a good choice none the less; it complimented the dish well,' I add.

Soon after we finish eating, people begin to leave their tables and head for the dance floor in the other room. We quickly follow; Sarah not wanting to miss a moment, leaving me to follow behind with Jim.

Jim sensing my apprehension, assures me I have nothing to worry about, as the steps are all explained and practised, along with the music.

'Just follow me. It's good fun,' he says, 'trust me!'

It's evident when we begin, it's in their blood—even the children don't need to be shown the steps. Sarah informing me they have been brought up doing this each year, and any other opportunity, more recently on the school playground. Whatever happened to the good old skipping rope!

I soon get the hang of things, listening for each do-si-do and remembering my left from my right. The perfect form of exercise after a heavy meal, hugely entertaining, with lots of hilarity. By eleven o'clock we are all exhausted, and the band finish with a Weaver's jig—something I was now familiar with. We bow and curtsey graciously to our partners before proceeding outside, Sarah staying to chat and help clear away. Henry bids goodnight and heads home, while Jim insists on walking me home, despite having had all that exercise! Saying, he would welcome the fresh air, explaining Sam wouldn't be back at Sarah's for a little while yet.

We wander slowly up the steep street, at times, feeling as though I'm still demonstrating the swagger step as performed earlier; no wonder Jim had insisted on walking me home! Not such a good first impression, considering Jim is still sober, having to drive home to be up early to milk the cows.

The road through the village is quiet in an evening, in fact any time of day. Most visitors choosing to park up at the top, rather than attempt the narrow winding street. All we can hear is the occasional owl, or music coming from the pub at the top of the hill. We chat easily, and as we approach my front door, I invite Jim in for a coffee, which he declines, assuring me he had thoroughly enjoyed the evening, expecting our paths would cross again soon. He ensures I find my key and unlock the door, before leaning towards me and putting his arm around my waist to kiss my cheek.

Chapter 4
Forever Green

It wasn't that long before I was to see Jim again, the following week Sarah had called to invite me over to spend some time with herself and the children. It had been a beautiful afternoon spent in the garden. She had asked me to stay and join them for dinner, mentioning her dad would be arriving later to join them. I wasn't sure, but got the impression it had been more of a plan than an impromptu invitation, wondering if Jim was aware of this.

The children fed, Sarah busied herself in the kitchen, preparing a feast for when Henry and Jim arrived, whilst I played quietly with the children. Henry arrived first, to the delight of his children. We all wandered back out into the garden to enjoy the now setting sun, Henry destroying all the hard work I had done to calm the children before bed, chasing them around the garden. There'll be tears before bedtime, as Sophie would say, but at least they would have sound lungs!

Sophie had been my nanny, almost from the day I was born. A local girl who had just finished college, wanting a career as a nanny, employed by my parents, continuing to care for me for the next eleven years, during which time she'd married and had two children of her own. I was an only child; my mother, not being the maternal type had been eager to return to work, so when I was just five months old, she'd done just that. Sophie had been good friends with Frank's mother and he and I had often played together after school, whilst they chatted over a cool drink in her beautiful garden. Sophie had been grateful for her advice, adopting many of her ways, her own garden began to resemble Frank's, filled with sweet smelling herbs, and her home smelt just as magical. Frank's mother had been a herbalist, full of green wisdom to treat common ailments. At the first sign of a cold, she would recommend hot elderflower and peppermint tea sweetened with honey, or, my favourite: hot water added to a dollop of homemade blackcurrant jam, always served in a beautiful china cup. Everything smelt so fresh and clean in her house, refusing to buy cleaning materials from the shop, she would simply add oils and herbs to the water to clean and disinfect, and use aromatic herbs to freshen a room. Her bathroom towels were thick and soft and always smelt of lavender, and her shelves held bottles of floral oils for bathing.

We continued seeing each other, and once I'd joined Frank a year later at secondary school, we'd walk to and from the bus each day together. The gate at the bottom of Frank's garden opened onto a track, leading down to the riverbank, another source of nourishment for the soul and body. The intoxicating scents in the summer sunlight awakening our senses, as we'd rowed our little boat across the river to our secret place that could only be reached by vessel, where we would light fires to keep us warm into the evening whilst reading Shakespeare to each other. We drank elderberry wine from the shed at the bottom of the garden, that nobody seemed to miss, whilst listening to 'Mike Oldfield's Tubular bells', boiled our own herbal concoctions to open our pores, to rid us of the awful acne, but never shared our first kiss. We had felt comfortable in each other's company, having been around each other from a young age, but as we grew, so had my feelings for Frank, never saying anything for fear of ruining our friendship. So as the years went by, our friendship became more awkward, no longer feeling comfortable around him. Frank started spending more time with the lads, whilst I was discovering my femininity with my female friends. When our paths did cross at a local party, we would avoid each other, uncomfortable in our platforms and perfume, drinking lager and lime. We continued growing apart; Frank started work in the city whilst I left for a life in a nanny role, many miles away.

Over the years my mum had never offered information about Frank. She had always made it obvious she had disapproved of our friendship; I never questioned her reasons or fought Frank's corner, still seeing him, regardless. So, when years later, she'd mentioned he had married, my whole world seemed to fall apart.

Jenny, who I was working for, and living with at the time in my role as a nanny, had found me sitting on the cold kitchen floor, leaning against the wall when she had returned with her husband George and the children later that evening, after being away for the weekend. Jenny had found the phone still in my hand and realised I must have been there for some time as I was cold and appeared to be in shock. George had cradled me in his arms and carried me up to bed, whilst Jenny had made me a cup of camomile tea—something we would give the children to comfort them, if the need ever arose. She had made me a hot water bottle and tucked me up in bed, sitting with me, ensuring I drank every last drop of tea, whilst trying to ascertain what had happened. I was unable to tell her, just nod when she had asked if it had been bad news, and sob uncontrollably. Jenny, relieved I was at least crying, had sat with me until I had fallen asleep, leaving me to wake naturally the next morning, having cancelled her meetings for the day. She had brought me breakfast in bed after taking the children to school herself, staying with me until I was able to pour my heart out to her, holding me whilst I sobbed some more. Despite having employed me as a nanny to look after her children, she was still a very good mother, and has remained a good friend to this day, eventually getting to know my dear Frank before he died, catching me when he did, and reminding me that love is immortal.

Lizzie ran past me shouting, 'Dandad!'

I turned to see Jim walking towards me, scooping Lizzie up in his arms and kissing her.

'This is a pleasant surprise, are you staying for dinner?' he asks.

'I am, Sarah asked me. I hope you don't mind,' I reply.

'Not at all, it's lovely to see you again,' he assures me.

Chapter 5
Sowing the Seeds of Love

The church bells beckon and the sun is starting to shine, as I turn the corner and make my way down the street towards the church. In the distance, I can see children arriving, carrying baskets of fruit and vegetables. As I near, it is evident I'm a little late, the church bells having ceased, and the lane emptied. Frank always said I was never on time for anything! I can hear Mary playing the organ as I open the heavy oak door, releasing an earthy mix of flowers and fruit. I immediately recognise the first hymn, even before the congregation starts singing. One we chose for your funeral, as God gathered you in with the harvest. I catch Jim's eye as he moves along the pew to make room for me. The service continues with readings, and a sermon encouraging us to look back at our lives, see what we are reaping now, and what plans we would like to plant for the future, at which point, Kate and Sam, who are sitting together, look into each other's eyes. I imagine we all know exactly what they're planning! The large oak door creaked open, allowing the children from the Sunday school to enter and fill the empty pews awaiting their arrival. The children brought with them corn dollies, which they make out of the last sheaves of straw. These were traditionally scattered and ploughed into the first furrow at sowing time, thought to encourage a plentiful harvest. The service so different to the ones I used to attend in the city, where children would bring tins of tomatoes from Italy and tuna from the Pacific Ocean to share with the homeless. Although a very Christian act, it isn't exactly celebrating a very important festival in the church calendar in the traditional way, performing the same rituals as those of their ancestors.

    The children I'd looked after in the city, would arrive home from school telling me all about other festivals celebrated around the world, unaware of all the activity they had just missed, happening not a million miles away, that I had been lucky enough to experience as a child. It was then that I'd decided to escape the city with them during the long summer holidays, to experience their own green and pleasant land, to run through fields of barley, visit a market to smell the fresh fruit and vegetables, or pick their own from the field or hedgerow, experiencing the fresh flavours and textures, growing in abundance, either left to rot, or for our prickly, furry or feathered friends to feast upon. The children delighting in what they discovered, away from the supermarket shelves providing them with imported, shrink wrapped, perfectly shaped food, whenever they desired. Each changing season bringing valuable foods appropriate to the time of year, food as nature intended.

During the war, American pilots were given instructions on how to live off the wild in case their planes were ditched over land. Here in the countryside, the government encouraged the hedge harvest as much as digging up your lawn to grow vegetables, publishing and distributing guide books to school children so they could identify and harvest common plants, providing them with an essential source of vitamins, no longer able to rely on imported produce. Now, many people would be unable to identify some of these plants, or their properties, instead, using their local chemist or supermarket to supply all their needs.

The service ended with Hymn number 375: "Jerusalem", and an invitation to Sunday lunch with Sarah and her family, which I accepted gratefully as I hadn't got up early enough to prepare anything myself, despite the extra hour in bed! We proceeded outside into a beautifully warm autumn morning, the sun shining on our dearly departed. People lingering to chat with each other and young children running in and out between the headstones, oblivious, as yet, to their ancestry beneath their feet, some long-forgotten distant relatives, as well as many young children who didn't survive childhood, and the odd individual who'd found themselves here, away from home. A little boy evacuated here in 1944, killed with his friend by an unmarked mine, the bodies of two friends here on holiday in 1970, aged just nineteen and twenty, both drowned, one courageously trying to save the other, and the course of true love that had brought my Frank, now resting in the field amongst the other loved souls.

Next week we will gather to remember all who fought in the armed forces and who never came home, a tradition still continued the length and breadth of the country, and in Ypres, where many lie where they fell in battle, in unmarked graves, known only unto God. A generation of young men lost, causing heartache and devastation, leaving those left to rewrite history.

A welcoming smell greeted us as Henry opened their rather quaint front door, adorned with a small wicker heart, quite appropriate considering all the love contained within the walls. The grate was empty in the hearth as Sarah directed Jim and I into the living room, whilst she finished preparing the lunch. Jim opened the wine, giving me a glass to enjoy along with the antics of Flora, one of his heifers, or gorgeous Holstein ladies, as he liked to refer to them, reckoning she must have gorged on more than her fair share of the apples given to them last night, as Harry had reported she wasn't quite herself this morning—normally wanting to be the first into milking—she had lagged behind, letting Tulip lead the herd. Harry had obviously got to know the personalities of these profound creatures, helping Jim on his farm, learning all there was to know before leaving school this year. Jim had now employed him full time to help Sam, allowing Jim to spend more time away from the farm and almost retire. Harry, lived on a neighbouring farm, the youngest of three sons; his older brothers already working on their family farm, and despite his young age, didn't mind getting out of bed in a morning! Jim, having now decided to finish work on completing the adjoining barn for him to live in, previously started several years ago now, as a future home for Sam one day. But after his mother had died it had fallen back into disrepair.

'Dad,' Sarah shouted. 'Do you want to bring Molly through? Lunch is ready.'

Sarah, had again produced another veritable feast for us all to enjoy. This family, of which I was almost beginning to feel part of, certainly ate well, and knew exactly which wine to serve to complement each meal. After lunch, Kate and Sam took Luke outside to play whilst Lizzie had a rest. Jim and I helped clear up with Sarah and Henry before retiring to the living room with the remainder of the wine, a most pleasant way to spend a Sunday afternoon. It wasn't long before Lizzie woke from her nap, and when Sam and Kate arrived back with Luke and normality resumed, Jim and I decided to leave. Although we both dearly loved the children, we were beginning to enjoy each other's company just as much.

The sun was already low as we strolled effortlessly up the hill towards home, where today, of all days, Jim accepted my invitation inside. My heart sank as I opened the door into my untidy home, having rushed out earlier, already late for church, not realising I would be inviting anyone back. Fortunately, I had managed to open the curtains before walking out of the door this morning. I apologise to Jim for any untidiness before inviting him into the kitchen where the breakfast pots still stood, casually slipping them into the dishwasher before filling the kettle. Hopefully he wouldn't notice, Frank would often say no one would. Although, I guess that may just have been his lazy streak! Either way, I was hardly creating the desired impression, first having to be escorted home last week, and now this! We carry our cups of coffee into the living room, now absent of any lingering daylight. I switch on the light and close the curtains as Jim sits down on the sofa, ideally placed for admiring all the photographs dotted around the room.

'Are these all your children?' he asks, in a startled voice.

'They're all the children I have cared for in my role as a nanny, before I moved here. Thirteen in total. I'm godmother to seven of them and to five of their children. This one's a picture of William Francis, Frank's grandson.' I say, handing him the framed photograph.

'Do you have any children of your own?' Jim continues.

'Unfortunately, not. It was too late when Frank and I eventually got together; we were both already fifty.'

'So not long ago then,' he says.

'Not long enough. But you can't always have everything the way you want in life,' I tell him. 'And nothing stays the same forever.'

'So how did you meet?' Jim asks.

'Oh, a long time ago! Frank was my best friend whilst we were growing up. I hadn't realised just how much I loved him until he was married. His marriage hadn't worked, and we met again at his mother's funeral, seven years ago,' I explain.

'Were you married?' Jim asks, now completely absorbed in my story.

'No, we never considered it necessary. We were happy regardless.'

'How long is it since Frank died then?' Jim asks, doing the sums.

'A whole year now,' I reply.

A few moments pass before Jim continues, 'My wife died several years ago now. A tragic accident, one Saturday morning whilst driving to get the papers. She should only have been gone ten minutes, but never came home,' he pauses. 'If only I'd known.'

'Would you like a drop of brandy in your coffee?' I ask, realising how upset he is.

'Thank you, that would be lovely,' Jim says, offering me his mug.

I return with his mug and the bottle, adding a tot to my own, before sitting back down and continuing the conversation, telling Jim about Frank's illness. 'Knowing the outcome had allowed me time to begin to accept the inevitable, although no amount of time could have been long enough to truly prepare me for life without him. I had been so absorbed in caring for him that I hadn't had much time to consider beyond that.'

Jim continues, 'I'm not sure the realisation is ever easy. I think I was lucky having Sam and Sarah. We all needed each other, still do. It's good to have them close by.'

I agree. 'I may not have the big family like you, but I've come to realise what amazing friends I've got.'

'That's obvious by the stack of cards out there! I assume it's your birthday tomorrow,' Jim enquires.

'You assume right.'

'Have you any plans?' he asks.

'No, none whatsoever. Frank had been the party animal.'

'Oh, I don't know about that. From what I've seen, some of that must have rubbed off onto you!'

'Would you let me take you out for dinner tomorrow evening?' Jim asks.

'I think I'd like that,' I reply. 'Thank you.'

'Talking of celebrations,' begins Jim, 'you know Kate and our Sam are getting married next month.'

'Yes,' I continue, interrupting him, 'Sarah is so excited and was telling me all about their plans. It sounds like it'll be a wonderful day.'

'Would you consider being my guest?' Jim asks me. 'I'd really enjoy sharing it with you.'

'Are you sure?' I reply. 'I haven't known you all that long.'

'Yes, I'm perfectly sure. I like what I do know, and everyone else feels the same. We already consider you as part of the family. We'd all be delighted if you accepted,' Jim concludes, 'especially me.'

'Well, as long as you're sure, I'd love to. Thank you. Two invitations in one day, and it's not even my birthday yet!' I add excitedly, before realising, that Jim, is actually the groom's father. 'Wait a minute! Doesn't that mean I'd be sitting on the top table?'

'Of course, next to me,' Jim says.

'But that doesn't seem right considering the short time I've known everyone,' I conclude.

'It's just etiquette who sits where,' Jim assures me, 'and besides, everyone else will be able to see the bride and groom, which is what they would prefer.'

'I suppose, but will you run it past Sarah?' I ask.

'It was her idea in the first place,' Jim continues, 'and before you ask, she has spoken to Kate and Sam, who are more than happy with it. So, all that remains is for you to talk to Sarah about a corsage for your outfit. I'm afraid I leave all that to her,' he admits. 'She reckons, after all the advice she has given Kate, she must be qualified to become a wedding planner,' he continues, 'Kate's mother works and hasn't wanted to be involved that much, so Sarah took on the role of helping Kate organise things. They get on well together.'

'That's good. Oh, I'm quite excited now!' I add. 'I'll talk to Sarah tomorrow. Are you hungry yet?' I ask Jim, and without waiting for a reply, invite him to follow me into the kitchen. 'Is a ham sandwich alright?' I ask. 'We did have a big lunch.'

'Thank you, that would be lovely. Yes, Sarah certainly knows how to cook, her mother taught her all she knows. She often reminds me of her, even when she makes a cup of tea, brewing it in a pot just like Lou showed her. I expect she will show Lizzie the same things as she gets older. Is your mother still alive?' Jim questions.

'No, she died several years ago, but therein lies another story,' I reply, giving Jim a plate of sandwiches and leading him back into the living room.

'I actually adopted many of Frank's mother's ways, perhaps spending more time with her whilst growing up, rather than my own. I always admired her and her lifestyle. She was a great influence on me, as I have been on the children I've cared for over the years. I would often take the children out of the city during their long summer holidays and share the familiar countryside I had taken for granted as a child. They marvelled in its beauty and enchantment, and relished in their freedom, loving every minute they were able to spend outdoors.'

Jim continues, 'You often don't appreciate what's under your own nose; it's only when you lose it, you realise what you had.'

'Unless you had to wait a lifetime,' I conclude.

'Perhaps you'll share it with me one day. You make it sound magical,' Jim comments, between bites.

'Would you like another cup of coffee?' I ask, changing the subject, unable to contemplate sharing something I hold so dear with someone else.

'I'm sorry,' Jim says, noticing my reluctance to acknowledge his suggestion, 'that was insensitive of me. Would you like me to go?'

'No, don't be silly, you haven't tried my chocolate cake yet!' I say, making a quick retreat into the kitchen to compose myself. Before I get chance to open the cake tin, Jim appears with his mug and plate. 'I must warn you, my chocolate cake isn't the best you'll have tasted. I make a wicked coffee and walnut sponge though, even if I say so myself!'

'If you don't mind, I think it's time I was going, I have to get up early with the children,' Jim sighs.

'It isn't that bad!' I insist. 'Of course, I didn't realise it'd got so late,' I say, looking across at the clock on the wall. 'Shall I still see you tomorrow?' I enquire.

'Yes, I'll let you know when I've booked a table. If that's all right?' he says.

'Thank you,' I reply, as we walk towards the door, whereupon Jim turns to kiss me tenderly on my cheek, wishing me goodnight before heading out into the cold, back towards the warmth of his family.

Chapter 6
Feeling Loved (and Tipsy!)

I woke after sleeping soundly, cocooned inside goose feathers. A few years ago, I would have jumped out of bed on my birthday, but today I'm happy to linger a little longer, reluctant to leave my duvet, relishing in the warmth. Eventually, I swing my feet out of bed, slipping on my pyjamas—something even I think odd—finding them too hot to sleep in, but perfect for lounging in. I wander to the end of the bed to open the curtains onto an already glorious day; the sun already up, as if in anticipation of the clocks changing next week. This week also brings the return of holiday makers, although not quite as many as during the summer months. There's now a growing percentage taking an October holiday, compared to years ago when people only took one holiday a year and perhaps an occasional long weekend. The majority now being second home owners returning to enjoy the last remnants of sunshine before shutting their properties up until next spring, having used up their holiday allowance for the year. I'm convinced many visitors wouldn't even recognise the picture postcard image they take away with them, were they to return during the winter months. Others simply choosing not to return, unable to associate the seaside out of the summer months. Fortunately, we don't attract many tourists, and certainly never the coach parties you see on the continent, processing through the narrow streets of quaint medieval towns, poking their lenses into their private lives, led by a lady with a flag!

I make my way downstairs, collecting my unopened cards and parcel from the top of the chest of drawers in the hallway, before entering the kitchen, which appears chilly this morning. I instinctively empty the kettle before filling it with fresh water for my morning coffee, something I had had instilled into me from when I first worked with a new born baby, adopting it myself. If it was good enough for a baby, then it was good enough for me! I decide to light the fire beside the table with the little bit of kindling and remaining logs from the basket. There had been no central heating in the house when Frank and I first moved in—just the fire in the kitchen, a stove in the living room and a small open fire in each bedroom. We both loved these features which we retained, but added a heated towel rail to the bathroom, which had taken priority over absolutely everything else, and within days of moving in had one ordered to be installed as soon as possible. Luckily for us, it was only October and we hadn't had to wait too long for what we then considered to be an essential. How on earth people managed with an outside toilet I'll never understand! We had also added a couple of wall-mounted electric heaters, one in the hallway and another on the landing, which to alter the temperature, is a little like reading Brail, feeling the notches to determine the heat setting as they are neither visible nor easily accessible, having left just enough room to slip your hand in to alter the setting, but nevertheless very effective in providing instant heat.

The kettle boiled, I empty some granola into a small, deep dish, which in another life had been designed as a sugar bowl, beautifully decorated with garlands of trailing roses, and a few hair line cracks, considerably out of proportion compared to the six, now four, dainty cups and saucers that remained. It had belonged to a part tea set I had inherited from Frank's mother, who never used sugar herself, sweetening her tea with honey or simply adding a slice of lemon. I imagine the bowl was more likely used for infusing herbs from her garden. Despite its age and fragility, I continue lifting it from the shelf on the dresser each morning, enjoying the luxury of eating my favourite mix of seeds from such an individual piece of antique china. Frank, on the other hand, had disliked my choice of breakfast, describing it as bird food! I refuse to be lazy, putting it in the dishwasher, choosing to wash it by hand to preserve the still very clear design. I pour the kettle, now at the optimum temperature to produce the perfect tasting coffee, and come to think of it, baby formula, in which case, if left for longer than thirty minutes should be discarded, the kettle emptied and filled again, as the water will have reduced in temperature, allowing it to develop harmful bacteria. By now, the poor baby who should have woken twenty minutes ago, is now wide awake and crying with hunger, whilst you empty the kettle down the sink and wait for it to boil again. I can't help but wonder what would be more detrimental to the baby's wellbeing!

I drench my granola in milk and carry it across to the table; the fire, now omitting a warm, comforting glow. I enjoy a spoonful before selecting the first envelope to open, choosing the one with a Lancashire postmark on it, recognising Sophie's perfectly formed handwriting, almost as if she has used a ruler. Inside the card is a sprig of lavender, still fragrant, taking me right back to her garden. I shuffle through the cards looking for one I received yesterday from Jenny and George, whom I have known from the start of my career. Jenny had been the one to comfort me after I had received the devastating news about Frank's marriage all those years ago, and again when Frank had been diagnosed, and not long after when he'd died. Inside was a beautiful card with a delicate lace design, almost like a fine piece of embroidery; even her Christmas cards were individually selected, and as beautiful. I open the next to reveal one from my oldest god-daughter Daisy, now with a family of her own. The doorbell rings before I have time to finish opening and displaying any more cards. Half expecting the postman with another delivery, I am surprised to see Jim standing there with Lizzie in one arm and a bunch of fragrant roses in the other.

'Happy birthday,' he chimes.

Luke adding, 'Mummy picked them from the garden for you, and I made you a card,' he continues, thrusting it towards me.

'Thank you Luke,' I say, accepting the card, still wet, unable to absorb the copious application of glue and glitter a young child deems necessary.

'I wasn't expecting to see you till this evening,' I declare, glancing down at my pyjamas. 'But come on in, you could probably all do with a drink if you've walked all the way here.' Without even looking at the clock I knew it must still only be nine o'clock, though realise this must equate to mid-morning to them. I expect it had been quite a while since they ate their breakfasts, something I would have to reacquaint myself with again quite soon.

Luke was already through the door and peering around, Lizzie fixed in Jim's embrace.

'Have you had to carry her the whole way?' I ask Jim.

'No, I've just lifted her from her pushchair, but Luke managed the whole way. Didn't you mate?' he addresses Luke, who is now on his knees surveying the glass cabinet behind the living room door, just as I remember doing myself as a child, each time I had visited my grandmother's house, transfixed with its beautiful contents, each with a story to tell, locked in time behind sparkling glass. The contents had been emptied, sorted, reintroduced and added to over the years since then. I had repositioned my favourite fine bone china lady, who epitomised a summers day—dressed in a beautiful lemon gown, holding a parasol over her shoulder; standing her exactly where I had remembered finding her, adding a sweet little bud vase, decorated with delicate lilac flowers, a favourite piece I remember from my childhood days, spent in and out of Frank's mother's house, that had previously stood on their mantelpiece, between the Clock and a framed picture of Frank as a young boy, now preserved for the next generation of children to admire.

Jim suggests he leaves with the children whilst I dress, and we meet halfway at the cafe for coffee. The children comply obediently, unable to resist the offer of a sweet treat. After shutting the door behind them I take the roses into the kitchen to place in my favourite cut glass vase: yet another heirloom of Frank's; my own mother preferring more of a statement Art Deco piece, without the flowers! I return to the living room to place the vase on the windowsill, along with some of the cards I had managed to open; it's then I remember the card Frank had written before he died last year, running upstairs to retrieve it from the drawer beside my bed, nestled in between the pages of the book I'd eventually finished reading to him. I open the drawer, but decide to leave it undisturbed, today unable to handle the sorrow. Something I have taught myself to do to remain strong. Instead, I turn to open the wardrobe to retrieve a freshly pressed blouse I have recently purchased for such an occasion. I pull on my jeans, twist up my hair and brush my teeth, not forgetting a spritz of my favourite perfume, bursting with fresh, vibrant, aromatic oils, guaranteed to awaken the senses. As always, I poke some earrings through my ears, continuing to add a sweet little necklace with a hanging swallow, that had arrived in the post from Grace. Slipping my feet into my ballet pumps, never knowing for sure what the weather has in mind, I head downstairs, grabbing my purse, before heading out through the front door. As I near the gate, a white feather drifts down ahead of me, stopping me in my track for a moment; I catch it and blow a kiss from whence it came, before slipping it into my pocket. My pace becomes leisurely now, allowing thoughts of Frank to enter my head; the feather, not the first to fall in the last year, but still few and far between, and when least expected. I continue past the hedgerows still laden with plump berries. The lane's quiet, despite the school holidays, although an odd vehicle or two parked outside the occasional property where there usually stands none. The bakery window is full of bloomers, farmhouse loaves, scones and a variety of other delicious cakes, which will all be sold by late afternoon. Before I know it, I've arrived at the little tea shop, freshly painted in a delicate shade of blue. Most businesses taking advantage of this time of year to maintain the upkeep of their buildings whilst the streets are quieter. Just inside the window are Jim and the children, Lizzie sitting in her pushchair holding a pale blue lidded beaker, almost certainly inherited from her brother, as no doubt are the Bob the Builder wellies on her feet, dangling from her short legs, none of which matters when you are just two! Jim noticing me, gets up to open the door.

'That was quick. We haven't been here that long ourselves. What can I get you?' he asks.

'A black coffee would be lovely, thank you,' I reply, as I hadn't had time to finish the one I'd poured earlier.

'I'm having a bacon sandwich; can I get you one?' Jim continues.

'Oh yes please,' I reply, without hesitation. 'I imagine I'm going to need it!'

Lizzie is now enjoying nibbling on a gingerbread man, whilst Luke is holding a small glass of milk between his hands, which he appears to be enjoying more than his biscuit! I remain quiet as I sit beside them, allowing them to relax and refuel. The shop is almost empty, but in just another hour, most tables will be occupied, especially now it's the school holidays, attracting the local children, offering somewhere warm and safe for them to meet, with a selection of healthy smoothies and milkshakes to tempt them.

It isn't long before Luke begins, 'We're going to the beach when we've had this.'

'Can I come too?' I ask, just as Jim returns to the table. Lizzie looks at Jim, unsure of his response.

'Do you like collecting shells?' Luke asks. 'Once, I collected loads!'

'And I collected loads too,' Lizzie adds.

'Well, perhaps we can have a competition to see who can collect the most,' I suggest. Unlike foraging, there is no limit on collecting what the tide washes in. 'Do you have some buckets?' Rather a daft question I suppose, to ask a small child who lives in such close proximity to a beach!

'Yes, do you have one Molly?' Luke asks me.

'I do, but it's in my shed at home. Do you have one I can borrow?' I reply.

'What colour do you want? Mine's red and Lizzie's is yellow,' Luke responds.

'Mine's yellow,' Lizzie repeats, accepting what her brother tells her.

'Do you have one Grandad?' I ask Jim.

'I'm sure there's enough for everyone,' Jim says, just as our bacon sandwiches arrive on a soft white bun, which we devour quickly.

'Right,' Jim says, 'is everybody ready to hit the beach?'

'Hit the beach!' Luke repeats, shortly followed by Lizzie!

We head off down the road, calling at Sarah's on the way to leave the pushchair and collect the buckets, spades and a towel, all quite manageable with two small children, each keen to carry their own bucket, leaving me with the orange one! You could, quite easily, arrive at the beach unprepared, and still manage to amuse yourself. The sun is now rising, and already starting to feel quite warm; the beach almost empty, apart from one young family already busy exploring the shallow rock pools, becoming more exposed with the retreating tide, often leaving little crabs behind. Luke and Lizzie run off excitedly, clutching the white handles on their plastic buckets, in search of the occasional shell, each one a fascinating find. Jim and I stroll silently behind, picking up the odd shell ourselves, languishing in the beauty of our surroundings, the warm sun, and our own thoughts. Mine of time spent here with Frank, who longed to spend each day down here, marvelling in all its majesty, invigorated and inspired with every fresh wave, until he grew too weary, then, like the departing waves, defeated.

'Grandad, look how many I've got,' Luke shouts, as he runs towards us.

'Should we count them?' Jim suggests, as Lizzie runs to join us, tipping out the shells she has managed to collect. Luke takes out each individual shell from his bucket, counting each one as he places it one behind the other on the sand.

'Ten!' he announces.

'Help Lizzie to count hers,' I ask Luke.

Luke separates the shells from the stones and declares he is the winner, without bothering to enquire how many Jim and I may have collected!

'Shall we wander back and collect the eggs and apples?' Jim suggests to Luke and Lizzie.

'Yes!' they both squeal, running away from the sea, leaving their wet footprints behind.

We wander slowly back up the lane until we reach the orchard, just to the side of their cottage, the trees' branches laden with fruit, ripe for the picking, before taking a well-deserved rest for the winter. Jim brings a few large baskets from the small shed at the far end of the orchard for the children to gather the bruised windfalls from the ground. As well as apples growing, there are other fruit trees: pears and plums. Jim reaches to retrieve a couple of pears, passing me one to eat, the smell so evocative, taking me back to Frank's garden as a child.

Perhaps noticing, Jim interrupts my thoughts, 'You've gone quiet again. What are you thinking? You were miles away earlier on the beach.'

'Oh,' I sigh, 'memories!'

'Happy I hope?' Jim enquires.

'And sad,' I consider.

'You can't feel one without the other,' Jim concludes.

'I'm sorry I've been a little distracted this morning. I promise to give you my full attention this evening,' I tell him.

'It'll get easier,' Jim assures me. 'You adapt. It almost becomes part of you. It's a little like recovering from a serious operation; it takes time to heal and regain your strength, but you will. We all do.'

He bends down to pick an apple from the ground to show Luke.

'Put any like this, in this basket,' he says, passing him an empty one. 'We'll give them Mummy to pickle.'

'Really?' I ask.

'Yes, they're crab apples; no good to eat as they are, not even the birds 'll touch them!' he explains.

Luke's suddenly distracted by two clucking hens approaching, alerting us of their presence, perhaps having been trodden on once too often!

'This is my hen, Molly. She lays eggs every day,' Luke explains. 'They're special because they're blue.'

'This is mine,' Lizzie declares, trying to catch the other.

'Lizzie's lays speckled eggs,' adds Luke.

We carry our buckets through a little gate that leads us to the garden, now in full sun and still displaying many beautiful blooms, despite the time of year, and having had the lovely bunch cut from this morning, though I suspect it won't be long before they are all stung by the first frost, which is when we'll be able to harvest the hips.

'Let's take the fruit and eggs inside,' Jim says. 'It won't be long before Mummy's home.'

Jim was right; soon after Sarah arrived.

'Hi everyone!' she chimes, announcing her arrival. Lizzie responding immediately, running to greet her mother, jumping into her open arms; embracing one another as though a long interlude has passed since they'd last seen each other. Whereas, Luke doesn't look up from the toys he is engrossed in playing with, completely absorbed in the moment.

'Happy birthday Molly! I've brought a cake back to have after lunch, if you'd like to join us?' Sarah asks.

'Thank you, I'd love that! I'm beginning to feel very spoilt! Let me come and help you in the kitchen; we can talk whilst Jim watches the children,' I say.

Sarah washes her hands, before passing me the serviettes and cutlery to take over to the table, whilst she empties the laden fridge of the previously prepared food, she'd obviously had to get up especially early to do. Although, having two small children, and growing up on a farm, I imagine she's no stranger to rising early.

'Dad told me he's invited you out tonight, and to the wedding,' Sarah says, whilst slicing a fresh crusty loaf.

'Yes,' I reply. 'Are you alright with that?'

'Of course! I would have suggested it myself if he hadn't. I've never seen him so happy in a long time; you're good for him.' Adding, 'Thanks for helping with the children today. They're becoming very fond of you, too.'

'I thoroughly enjoyed it. I'm always happy to help,' I reply.

We continue chatting about the wedding preparations whilst we all share lunch: another veritable feast of cold fish, local cheeses and a huge bowl of cold conchiglie and vegetables dressed with fresh mint from the garden and a jug of dressing. Sarah also insisted we celebrated with a glass of sparkling wine to accompany the cake: a huge vanilla sponge, beautifully decorated with white royal icing and large pink flowers with yellow centres dotted around the sides, filled with vanilla buttercream and strawberry jam. After which we were instructed to relax with a cup of coffee and the tin of biscuits! It is remarkable that none of this family are the size of houses, the amount they are fed, whereas they all look very lean and healthy. I certainly won't need to eat again until this evening.

Jim and I are dismissed, allowing me to return home to relax and pamper myself before being spoilt again, and for Jim to go and check on his precious girls, promising to be back to collect me at seven this evening. With an hour or so to spare before indulging in my bathing ritual, I continue opening my cards, something I prefer to spend time enjoying, rather than rushing, appreciating the thought that has gone into each and every one of them. I carry the cards with me on my journey upstairs, having already filled the window ledges downstairs. I place the remainder on the landing and my bedroom window ledges, brightening up the whole house and reminding me I'm loved. As well as the cards, I've remembered to bring some milk in a small china milk jug, on a slightly smaller scale, and different design to the bowl I ate from this morning. Milk, I've found, is an excellent medium for distilling and dispersing essential oils into my bath, also a softening agent, soothing the skin. I would have to ask Jim if the milk straight from his cows would be more beneficial. My bathtime has, over the years, become quite a ritual, requiring a little preparation, but well worth the while. Before I do anything else, I turn on the towel rail, not forgetting to add a large, soft white towel that, when heated, omits its lavender aroma and memories of Frank, who insisted I launder the towels just the way his mother had, adding lavender oil to the final rinse. The bathroom itself is a complete haven of tranquillity, still retaining some of the original features: a whitewashed stone wall, despite it being uneven. Unable to fix anything to it, we'd placed a free-standing old dresser we'd found in an antique shop window against it, perfect for holding my selection of essential oils and flower vinegars. In other jars are peppermint tea bags, a refreshing treat for tired feet, and camomile to soothe the emotions. Above these is a small jar of clover honey, the bees already having added the herbs, and a bottle of almond oil. Standing on the window ledge is a jar full of herbs infusing in the sun, and a clock on the wall, so I don't lose all track of time. In many ways, not dissimilar to my kitchen, containing all the necessary ingredients to nourish the skin and soul, preferring to use what nature intended, sustainable, wild and organic ingredients. Supporting the communities that harvest these precious oils when I can't harvest them myself, enriching their lives, as they are mine.

    I hang my robe on the hook behind the door before switching on the taps, adding just five drops of frankincense oil to the tiny jug of milk before pouring it into the running water, adding a liberal squirt from a bottle of baby shampoo, an essential element as far as I'm concerned, unable to enjoy a bath without any bubbles. I light a candle, not only to enhance the now dwindling daylight, but to intensify the aroma, allowing me to completely relax, lifting all my cares away with the smouldering oils, along with a prayer to my angel in heaven. Submerged in tranquillity, I realise there is nothing more reviving than the sensuous pleasure of relaxing in warm aromatic bubbles. Well worth all the initial suffering Frank and I had had to initially endure before creating this little haven of tranquillity.

    Once revitalised, I emerge, wrapping myself in the now warm towel, dabbing my feet on the thick piled bathmat, leaving the door open, allowing the aroma to penetrate throughout the entire house before entering my bedroom to dress; the room now warm and cosy. I choose pretty, matching underwear: a favourite set of mine, that I don't wear every day; one I had had to purchase whilst away in Bruges, having forgotten to pack another, just unfortunate I hadn't found it on my own high street! My grandmother had always said, one should never leave the house without wearing clean underwear; I insist it also has to be pretty, matching underwear. Rumour had it, my auntie hadn't taken any notice of her mother, displaying none at all during the summer months!

Having already mentally selected my outfit whilst waking yesterday—something I have learnt to do, leaving my head clear to sleep at night, it is all ready and waiting. An outfit I had bought for a summer wedding last year, that Frank had still been able to enjoy with us, all be it one of the last. The floral dress: smart but casual, reminiscent of the fifties, tucked in at the waist with a full skirt, along with a cropped red cardigan, hung, together on the same hanger, something else I had learnt to do over the years, rather than wracking my brain as to what to wear with each piece. Or worse still, not being able to find what I wanted, without emptying my entire wardrobe! My shoes, I keep in the bottom of my wardrobe, in their own original boxes with the contents on view, written on the sides, so I don't have to open each box to retrieve the pair I am looking for. I even had the perfect bag, bought to complete the outfit, the only difference being, the lack of a corsage to denote my destination. Tonight, I wasn't even going to need an umbrella, the sun now having set on a beautiful day. I spritz my perfume onto my wrists, just as my grandmother had taught me when I was a young child, rubbing my wrists behind each ear. I open my jewellery box sitting on my dressing table, as it has since my sixteenth birthday, a present from my parents, along with a gold, heart shaped locket, containing a picture of my grandfather, and father as a young child, having belonged to my grandmother, who had requested it be given to me on my sixteenth birthday. I adored it and had hidden a picture of Frank behind the picture of my father, which has remained there ever since. I take off the necklace I'd received this morning, choosing to wear just a pair of simple, but very special earrings: pink sapphires, each set in a gold star, a gift from Frank a few years ago. I can't help but think of him when I put them in my ears, sometimes unintentionally twisting them, reminding me of him. I add to this a ring, this time a white gold band with a single pink sapphire standing between a diamond on either side, which over the years, as I changed shape, began to fit perfectly on my wedding finger, which Frank had liked. We both knew how each other felt, not needing a ceremony or certificate to confirm it. Then a bracelet, this time without a hallmark, but containing vibrant pink stones in every link, that works perfectly with this and many other outfits, something I had bought myself, many years ago to wear with a ball gown, quite expensive, but worth every penny. I fill my bag with the few essentials a girl needs, not forgetting my glasses to read the menu.

Jim arrives punctually, as arranged. I open the door to an even more dashing gentleman, who smells as good as he looks, appearing to have made as much effort as myself for this evening. He compliments me on my appearance, as I do him, as he opens the door of the car in which Sarah is waiting to drive us to our destination, less than a mile away, allowing Jim to have a drink and celebrate with me.

'Enjoy your evening,' Sarah shouts, after we have thanked her.

Jim, having impeccable manners, opens the door for me into the warm, inviting pub—a restored seventeenth century inn, full of charm and steeped in history, most of which depicted on its walls, nestled in a beautiful, secluded cove, attracting passing tourists as well as the locals, both for a drink and a meal. But, unknown to many, hosts lavish dining and sitting rooms above the bar, as well as bedrooms. We head to the bar where Jim explains to the young man that he has booked a table for dinner. We order our drinks and carry them up the narrow, winding staircase, leading to lots of cosy little rooms. We find an unoccupied sitting room where the fire is lit, sinking into a plump, olive green, velvet sofa beside each other. We are given the menus and wine list to peruse whilst each drinking a Kir Royal to celebrate my birthday. The menu is varied, the chef priding himself on using local produce, all grown, raised and landed here, always having an abundance of fresh fish to choose from. Jim is attracted to the duck, served with a marmalade gravy, something I would never have dreamt of combining. As always, I choose the scallops for my starter—this evening: pan fried with lemon grass and ginger. Jim informing me that scallops are like trees, representing their age by the rings on their shells, and can live well into double figures, although, best harvested and eaten between three and five years old, whilst succulent and sweet. The wine list is extensive, offering something for every palate and dish, although not to everyone's pocket, favouring more characterful bottles than one might afford downstairs to compliment the pub grub. I love reading the description of wines; if it was up to me, I would choose a bottle on the description alone. We each decide to choose a glass to complement our own dishes, Jim choosing a Burgundy, with complex aromas of violets, earth and spice, boasting ripe, exuberant black cherry notes, with hints of forest undergrowth and a long-lasting finish. While I decide on what has become a favourite of mine since first discovering it, the very first time Frank and I visited here: a delicately flavoured white, with apricot and green fruit aromas, the perfect accompaniment to fish, celebrating the Atlantic Ocean in a glass.

The dining room reminds me of my grandmother's house, polished oak furniture, ornate china table lamps, standing lit on sideboards around the room, adding to the ambiance. White linen cloths and serviettes adorn each table, set with silver cutlery and cut glass. The windows are hung with sumptuous drapes, reminiscent of the period portrayed, the ultimate in refined luxury. There are another two tables occupied, and from over Jim's shoulder I can see a couple, a little younger than ourselves, sitting opposite each other. Again, waiting to be served, but may as well have been on their own for all the attention they are paying each other, more interested in reading other people's news on their phones than sharing their own with each other. What a shame, when they have chosen such a beautiful setting to dine together. Jim and I on the other hand, who given our age and the fact we are both wearing rings, may appear a married couple, though our acute interest in one another, perhaps says otherwise.

After our meal, we decide to order some cheese to share, along with a glass of port each—perfumed, enchanting and dangerously drinkable! Along with the selection of Cornish cheeses are, biscuits, grapes, celery and nuts, which we continue to enjoy along with each other's company. We finish with a decaffeinated filter coffee, served with a dark chocolate truffle.

Jim having already ordered a taxi to arrive in fifteen minutes, settles the bill, which includes a discretionary one-pound donation for the RNLI, to help save lives at sea.

Jim suggests we go back to Sarah's, the night still being young, but instead arrive at mine, imagining Sarah has probably seen enough of the pair of us for one day! Once inside, Jim comments, 'Your house smells almost of you!'

'And probably will do, well into tomorrow,' I assure him. 'I hope you like it then!'

'I love it, though I'm not sure if it's this, or the wine sending me high!'

'High, or relaxed?' I ask, as I light the candle I had intentionally brought down from the bathroom before I went out earlier, to enhance the mood.

'Content,' Jim concludes.

'Good. Brandy or bubbles?' I enquire.

'I know your partial to your bubbles, and it is after all your birthday.'

'The right answer,' I reply, returning with two flutes, and the chilled bottle Jim had presented me with earlier. I put on a CD of mixed tracks, one of several compilations I enjoy, with or without company. Accepting my glass from Jim, we continue to chat. Despite having already consumed several glasses of alcohol over the course of the day, I pour another generous amount into each of our glasses, not that Jim refuses! My hand still steady, I aim for the centre of the very narrow opening, something I am proud of having only mastered in recent years, before, appearing tipsy, when it dribbled down the side of the glass. The tempo changes and I get up and offer Jim my hand. 'Dance with me,' I exclaim.

Jim looks at me a little bewildered for a moment, then accepts my plea, embracing me and the moment. I nestle my head into Jim's warm chest, the heady aroma and the alcohol now engulfing my whole body. I can feel Jim's pounding chest, raising my face towards him, our lips touch, then caress more fervently, gently lingering into the next track, my whole body now pulsating.

'I've been wanting to do that since I danced with you at the village hall,' Jim says softly, 'but was afraid. In fact, I think it's perhaps time I head back to Sarah's for the night.'

'I don't understand,' I question.

'You will in the morning,' Jim replies, as he heads towards the door. 'Goodnight Molly.' Jim turns, not looking back as he walks out into the night.

Chapter 7
Lest We Forget

This evening was the next time I was to see Jim, the first time since my birthday, although he had called the very next day, later in the morning to be precise, to check I was well and if I perhaps needed anything bringing from the nearest largest city, still miles away to have to venture out to, too often. Jim explained he was going to collect his suit for the wedding, enquiring as to the colour I had chosen to wear, so he could choose a tie accordingly. Sarah had also asked Jim to ask me to call her regarding a corsage for the wedding, now less than two weeks away. I had reassured Jim that I was up and about and well, despite having drunk so much! Choosing to ignore his sudden departure the night before, instead, discussing the colours in my outfit and what he might consider appropriate for himself. Jim had failed to invite me to join him on his excursion, not that I would have accepted, still feeling a little delicate, but it would have been nice to have been asked. He did however remind me, that I had agreed to spend Friday evening helping him look after Luke and Lizzie, whilst Sarah and Henry went along to the annual firework display, and then on to a party nearby. I had agreed, as I had no intention of going to the display on my own, the excitement of which, had long eluded me.

For the vast majority of the week, I had remained confined to my kitchen, preparing fruit for mince pies and Christmas cakes, lining tins and baking, a process, once started, must be seen through to the end. A little ahead of schedule; Frank's mother having instructed me that once bonfire night was over, to turn my attention to Christmas preparations in the kitchen—I had discovered, that an extra week, not only enhanced the flavour, but also meant I had more time to address other unforeseen eventualities that always seemed to present themselves. Having only ventured out briefly for fresh ingredients to nourish me, rather than replenish the larder, having bought what I needed the last time I had done a big shop. Not having the convenience of a local supermarket, I had become more organised since living here, just buying fresh local produce as and when I needed.

Our kitchen had been old and basic when we had first moved here, so after completing the bathroom, we had sat down and designed the space around our needs, first and foremost a coffee machine for Frank, who loved the taste and aromas from freshly ground beans, and a spice drawer for me, to lay down my favourite ingredients, like Frank's fine bottles of wine. Despite the addition of a few modern appliances, we had still managed to retain its character.

By the end of the week the house oozed sugar and spice, and the beginning of Christmas. I did of course make a batch of mince pies, one of which I enjoyed warm with a cup of tea before taking some out with me to leave with Sarah to enjoy.

Jim opens the door with Lizzie in his arms, dressed for bed and holding onto her beloved ragged brown bear with her thumb in her mouth. Luke, I can hear behind the living room door, engaged in animated play, quite happily, if not preferably on his own, a little self-conscious perhaps in his grandad's presence, just as I am stood in front of him, remembering the last time I had seen him. As ever he smells divine, despite having spent the entire week on the farm, not once have I seen him in his farming attire.

'Lizzie's tired so I'm just taking her up to bed, I'll be down in a few minutes.'

'Night-night, Lizzie,' I whisper softly, as they brush past me towards the stairs.

I peep around the door, so as not to startle Luke, still engrossed, until he notices me, introducing me to the characters in his hands, explaining their roles in his story. Jim joins us, and Luke explains, 'When Grandad looks after us, he lets me stay up longer than Lizzie because I'm older and I go to school now.'

'Yes, I know,' I say, continuing the conversation, completely at ease with Luke, but still rather uncomfortable in his grandfather's presence.

'Can I get you a drink Molly?' asks Jim.

'Oh, what are you having?' I ask.

'Milk,' replies Luke. 'I always have a glass of milk before I go to bed.'

'That'll make you big and strong,' I tell him. 'What else is there? I'm not quite ready for bed!'

'There's a bottle of red been opened earlier,' Jim informs me.

'That sounds lovely, thank you,' I say, starting to relax.

'What's red?' asks Luke.

I begin explaining the different complexities of wine to Luke before Jim returns with a couple glasses of Merlot. Luke squashes between Jim and me on the sofa with his cup of milk and a book to share—not your normal bedtime story, a more interesting read about wildlife, animals to be exact. Luke, not content with just basic recognition and acceptance of these creatures, but curious to gain a deeper understanding of their behaviour and species, from slugs and snails to hedgehogs and seals. Tonight, was the turn of the tiny, plump dormouse with its appealing big brown eyes, long furry tail and whiskers, stuffing hazelnuts and blackberries into his bulging cheeks, a final feast to sustain him through the winter before curling up to hibernate. Not quite as appealing as the description of Thomasina Tittlemouse, wearing an apron and bonnet, portrayed by Beatrix Potter. Luke delighting in their existence, unfortunately, as a child I hadn't shared the same appreciation, taking for granted the daily dawn chorus, unable to distinguish between the birds singing. The bright blue kingfishers darting up stream, past the heron standing guard each day waiting for his dinner, probably as oblivious to me, as I was them, accepting their presence and the changes happening all around me, instead of realising how fortunate I was to witness all these beautiful things.

Roald Dahl once said, '...watch with glittering eyes the whole world around you because the greatest secrets are always hidden in the most unlikely places. Those who don't believe in magic will never find it.'

'Daddy said,' Luke began, 'he had a hamster when he was little. I might get one.'

Jim responding almost immediately, 'They may want to sleep most of the day, rather than play, some animals do.'

Luke looking a little bewildered, asks, 'Can I take my book upstairs? I've got a torch now, so I can read in bed, like Mummy does.'

'That's a good idea,' Jim agrees. Luke already clambering onto Jim's back, grabbing hold of his book. I wish him goodnight as they leave the room.

I sit back and enjoy another sip of wine, soothing and mellow, a perfect choice, especially sat on Sarah's cosy sofa in front of the now glowing fire, far preferable to the celebrations happening outside.

Jim returns, putting some music on before adding a couple of logs to the fire, remaining on the floor, leaning against a chair with his legs outstretched in front of me. We exchange pleasantries, enquiring about each other's week since we last saw each other, neither of us mentioning his abrupt departure. Jim stands to retrieve the bottle to top our glasses up, each taking another sip. He returns the bottle to the chest of drawers behind us, placing his glass on the mantelpiece before turning and extending his arm towards me, inviting me to join him, embracing me as we begin to sway together to the music, my face against his warm pulsating chest, his arms gently caressing my back. I lift my head, our eyes, then lips meet, engaging in a long and passionate kiss. No longer hesitant, Jim's kisses become more urgent as he begins unfastening the buttons on my blouse.

We lie together in each other's arms in front of the now ebbing flames, gently kissing one another, silent and satisfied under a blanket Jim had retrieved from the arm of the sofa, only to be disturbed by Jim's phone, which he had left on the little table beside the sofa along with my wine. He manages to reach it whilst still preserving his dignity, reassuring Sarah that the children are both asleep in bed and wishing her a good night. Returning to my embrace, we begin kissing again, before discussing a more romantic retreat without any distractions.

Jim dresses and then leaves the room, suggesting we reconvene in the kitchen, where I find him stood between the island and the grill, watching the cheese bubble on top of the toast, whilst adding hot milk to a bowl of what appears to be melted chocolate.

'What's all this?' I ask.

'Here!' Jim says, handing me a whisk, 'give that a good whisk.'

As if by magic the mixture starts to thicken and froth, as Jim produces bubbling cheese on toast from under the grill. We carry our supper back to the living room and sit beside each other on the sofa, both nibbling and sipping, taking me back to my childhood, and just right for a chilly evening. Now late, and Sarah and Henry still not expected home for a couple of hours, Jim and I retire to what is known as "Grandad's bedroom". It had been decided, rather than walking home on my own, I would sleep in the guest bed and Jim would sleep on the sofa. Jim had texted Sarah explaining the situation, so she wouldn't be alarmed to find her father slumped on the sofa.

I wake the next morning to the pitter-patter and squeals of young children across the landing, at the same time my phone beeps with a text from Jim, asking me to let him know when I was awake. No sooner have I replied, there is a knock on my door. Jim peeps in, and on seeing I am awake, closes the door behind him, before jumping on the bed beside me. 'I'll see you downstairs,' he says, before leaving me to shower.

Downstairs Sarah is cooking a full English breakfast for us all. It seemed her late night had only added to her enthusiasm for the day, ever grateful for the chance to party. Henry, however, seems to be a little more fragile, but enjoys his breakfast all the same, as do Luke and Lizzie, both dipping their sausages into their eggs. Breakfast being just another occasion to gather and relax, to enjoy family time together; this morning, after the plates have been cleared, there are warm croissants and continuous coffee to accompany the conversation about the impending wedding, just a week away now. Jim being less involved this time, as father of the groom. Kate, Sam and Sarah having arranged and organised almost everything themselves; Kate's mother picking and choosing what she's wanted to be involved in, allowing her more time to choose her own outfit, though she had agreed that guests be allowed back to their house for afternoon tea, just as long as outside caterers supplied the food and drink, and waiters and waitresses were on hand to administer everything. Reminding me of my own mother, and how she would have behaved if the opportunity had ever arisen, always delighting in being invited to social occasions, having the opportunity to dress to impress, not that I remember her hosting such events, let alone a birthday party for her own daughter! Christmas had either been a quiet affair at home, or more usually at friends or relations. The wedding was to be held a few miles from here at Kate's local church at eleven am, allowing them to make the most of the dwindling daylight bestowed upon us at this time of year. They had chosen November, it being the quietest time in the dairy farmer's calendar, with the herd now in the barns, and calves not due till the spring. Jim, it seemed, was quite looking forward to stepping into the breach and getting his hands dirty again.

Our shoes were polished, outfits hung, cards written and presents wrapped, as well as a few notes enclosed in the card as requested. Like many couples getting married today, they have already set up home together, therefore not needing the essentials like young couples of my generation, needing everything from a potato peeler to a hoover, having saved during their engagement for a house of their own, not moving in until the bride was carried over the threshold. Whereas couples these days, may already have all the material things for the home, but have had outgoings every month, with little left to save for a rainy day or honeymoon, which is why Jim had paid for them to have a week away. Their plan being relaxation and luxury within grounds to stroll and enjoy—nothing too energetic, and not too much travelling between. Starting with two nights in a luxury country house hotel, set within a hundred and twenty-seven acres of grounds, renowned for its luxurious spa rooms and one of the best chefs in the country—not that far from home; recommended by Kate's parents, having celebrated their own pearl wedding anniversary there recently.

Once suitably refreshed, Jim and I had left and headed home, as I'd needed to change, unsuitably dressed for exploring the outdoors, not having envisaged staying over. Once home, we had in fact remained indoors for the best part of the day before acquiring an appetite—supressed by a risotto, rustled up from some ingredients in the fridge, including wine, leaving just enough for a large glass each to accompany the dish. Jim had left quite early the following morning after we had fallen into a beautiful sleep in each other's arms.

The bells were ringing out as I made my way towards the church, unlike all those years ago, when silenced, not knowing if the next time would be to signal invasion or victory. I opened the gate and made my way up the path through the graveyard, passing the memorial for all the men and boys who never returned home, only twenty-eight villages eventually saw all their men return from the First World War, unfortunately ours wasn't one of them. The graveyard is full of courageous people, including those who suffered as a result of the conflicts; one of the headstones simply reads, "love never dies". The suffering this church, and many others must have seen as a result, is unimaginable. Barely a family in the land was unaffected by the devastation on the Somme, nearly half a million soldiers losing their lives between July and November. Twenty thousand on the first day alone!

As always, I arrive just in time to pick up my hymn book from just inside the door before the congregation stands to sing the first hymn, number 380: "I vow to thee my country". The church today a lot fuller than usual, as they no doubt will be up and down the country, year after year, filled with young and old remembering the sacrifices made. I make my way quietly towards the bench where I normally sit with Jim, who catches my eye, indicating a space beside him at the end of the pew. As ever he is smartly dressed, but today with the addition of a tie and jacket. I myself am wearing my tailored coat I'd brought with me from the city, perfect for such an occasion, especially as we gather outside, along with many others, again, up and down the country, to pay our respect to the gallant men who lost their lives. If we stood in silence for every Gurkha who fell in world war two, we would have to remain quiet for two weeks! The silence is broken by the resounding "Reveille", traditionally played on the bugle, today and for the last few years played on trumpet by Oliver, the teenage son of a regular parishioner, before we make our way sombrely back into the warmth of the church. The service continues with Hymn number 383: "O valiant hearts", sounding beautiful, and perfectly played by Mary, despite her cold fingers. As ever there are a few notices at the end, concluding today on a happier note—the final reading of the banns for Kate and Sam's marriage.

'Will you join us for lunch, Molly?' Sarah asks, as we spill outside.

'I was rather hoping you would ask, I'd love to. Thank you,' I reply.

Chapter 8
Till Death Do Us Part

The day of the wedding arrived. For Kate, it must have been like waiting for Christmas day as a child. I can only imagine the emotions she must be feeling right now, despite demonstrating calm under pressure. Even when the veil had failed to be ordered, accepting the one from the showroom as her something old, too late to have ordered another.

As well as being a godmother, I had also been a bridesmaid, but unlike the saying "always a bridesmaid never the bride", this had only been the once when I had been a lot younger, to a friend from school, who like me had no sisters of her own. Her mother, like mine, had worked and we had become soulmates, sharing our adolescence, experiences, clothes and aspirations, until she married and devoted her time to her husband. Although we were never as close as we had once been, we still to this day remain in contact.

Today Kate was to have her two younger sisters following her down the aisle, both wearing identical navy-blue satin gowns. My gown, had been a lilac, floral design, chiffon, tiered dress, with short puffed sleeves, typical of the eighties, still in its original box in the loft—what on earth for, I have no idea! Just one of those things that gets kept for sentimental reasons. Now, I should imagine, it would be more at home in a museum than on a bridesmaid, though would still have to be donated! It now sits beside a few other boxes my father has recently given me to sort through, that had belonged to my mother, perhaps the intention being I would discover my paternity, rather than having to now explain. Other than that, the loft remains virtually empty, never accumulating much myself, having lived in other people's houses. The few things my mother did keep from my childhood, including a beautiful scaled down replica of a Silver Cross pram with a navy folding hood and shopping basket, now retro, I eventually left with Tilly, realising I would probably never have the pleasure of seeing my own daughter play with it.

Despite getting to know Kate and Sam over the last couple of months, I still felt a little uncomfortable sharing such an important occasion with them and their lifelong friends and relations, but Jim had assured me otherwise. After all, there would be partners of other guests that would be in a similar situation to myself, although they wouldn't be sitting down at the top table! Jim was aware of my concerns, pointing out, it was only right that he too had a guest to share the day with, promising to look after me.

I stand in front of the mirror in the hallway to apply my lip-gloss and fix my hat, not quite sure as to what angle the designer had quite envisaged it being worn, hoping I did it justice, and that it would remain exactly in place for the entirety of the day. Suddenly, remembering my ring I'd left beside my bed, I negotiate the stairs with my heels and hat, remembering to lower my head just as Frank had had to do, to his annoyance!

The doorbell chimes just as I reach the bottom of the stairs. I open the door to be greeted by an admiring smile, a kiss on the cheek and, 'Wow, you look amazing!' Just what I needed to hear! As expected, Jim is standing there smarter than ever, complete with a white rose bud and a sprig of lavender in his buttonhole, along with an admiring smile and a similar arrangement of flowers for myself, but with the addition of what I'd described to the florist as a coral coloured rose to add warmth to the pale colours in my outfit. His smart grey Land Rover, I noticed, was gleaming, inside and out, as he opened the door.

Sam was already standing outside the church with his best man Guy, almost unrecognisable in their tails and polished shoes. Sarah, Henry and the children were the next to arrive; the children looking adorable, Luke in his navy three-piece suit and Lizzie in a similar coloured tailored wool coat with a matching cloche felt hat, reminiscent of the roaring twenties, with grey stockings to keep her legs warm and her black patent, laced ankle boots she had been so proud to show me, marching up and down the landing like she was on the red carpet.

Despite Sarah always looking glamorous, even in her jeans, she looked even more stunning today, having wanted so hard to support her brother and Kate, no doubt missing her mother today. Guy, was in charge of keeping the ring safe, Sam's mothers ring, given to him by Sarah after Jim had given it to her following her mother's death, a beautiful eighteen-karat gold band that Kate had once admired and wanted to replicate. Sarah, already married, had seen no reason why her brother shouldn't give it to his bride, and happily volunteered it, Kate, honoured to be able to receive and wear it, promising to cherish it.

The guests started arriving, like animals to the ark, congregating outside the little church, along with the photographer, catching fleeting moments before the ushers ensured everyone was escorted to their seats before the arrival of the bride and her father.

Jim and I sat eagerly awaiting their arrival, announced by Kate's mother, being the last to take her seat before the wedding march began. We all stood and turned to watch Kate proceed down the aisle, arm in arm with her father. Reaching Sam, he kisses his daughter's hand before giving it to him; Sam, accepting it tenderly, holding onto it throughout the entire ceremony. Kate, looking absolutely beautiful in her elegant lace gown and trailing veil, as did the church, the entrance and alter beautifully decorated with large blooms of Hydrangeas, and smaller adornments of gypsophila, roses and ribbon on the end of each pew, the sunlight beaming through the coloured panes of glass.

The ceremony was traditional, as Kate and Sam had wanted all along, finishing with "Love Divine": Jim's suggestion, as he and Sam's mother had used it, to conclude their wedding. We follow the bride and groom out of the church and into the sunshine where they are showered with various petals, captured on many cameras and kissed by many loved ones, before being captivated by the unassuming photographer, keen to get photographs whilst the sun shines. Jim shakes his son's hand, telling him his mother would have been proud of him, of course he was going to miss her on their son's wedding day. The family are called to take their positions in front of the church for the obligatory photographs. Despite being made very welcome into their family life, I still didn't regard it my place to stand and have my photograph taken alongside other family members, when they would want to look back and remember their mother, deliberately keeping my distance, hoping I wouldn't be noticed, thus avoiding any unnecessary conflicts.

After a brief shoot, the bride and groom depart, ahead of the rest of the congregation for the short journey to a magnificent hotel, with no less than a mile-long driveway, running between stunning conifers and shrubs, which I imagine would be beautiful all year round. The hotel, once it comes into view, doesn't disappoint either, with formal gardens in front and either side of the terraced steps leading up to the entrance, where you can't resist turning to admire the setting, before entering the very grand reception area, from where we are escorted past a sweeping staircase and through into a large period sitting room, adorned with portraits, fine porcelain and antique furniture. Inside, there are waiters waiting with Champagne for each and every guest, allowing us time to mingle whilst the bride and groom are again with the photographer, making the most of the daylight and beautiful setting before the celebrations begin. Jim is very attentive and happy to introduce me as Molly, no more, no less, allowing everyone to draw their own conclusions, all the time paying close attention to who I was being introduced to, only able to remember odd ones, hopefully the right ones: Pat with the pink hat, Agnes with the loud dress, and of course Sarah's grandma, her mother's mother. Occasionally, I'd sense penetrating eyes behind my back, or catch an occasional whisper or nudge from the odd guest, who I gathered were either curious or disgruntled relatives, including Kate's mother; Jim had obviously met her before, and if my eyes weren't mistaking me, she was almost flirting with him, in front of both me and her husband! Jim cast me a wink of reassurance before returning his attention to the mother of the bride. I got the impression Jim was fully aware of her attention and it was nothing new. After all, he was an exceedingly attractive man, but no longer eligible, which she had either failed to recognise or chosen to ignore. I was certainly going to mark her card.

It wasn't long before Jim was acquisitioned by Sarah, who subsequently commandeered me. Apparently, the photographer, who had obviously been informed of our situation, was now ready to photograph us together, as instructed I imagine, by Sarah. Jim obviously comfortable with the idea, holding me close with his arm around me.

As we make our way back inside, Jim says, 'I'm sorry you had to witness that before.'

I raise my eyebrows, responding, 'I can see I'm going to have to keep an eye on you two!'

'I've never encouraged her, and besides she's married!' he comments, hoping to reassure me, giving me a quick kiss before we're summoned to the table, almost like entering a courtroom, awaiting trial, on full display for everyone to scrutinise, which doesn't really worry me as I know none of these people, but had vowed to be on my best behaviour and adhere to the required etiquette.

The food was exquisite; the main—a hearty dish, the wine flowing freely, Kate and Sam had chosen well! Our glasses were charged, and the speeches began, starting with Kate's father, full of pride for his eldest daughter, who in turn handed over to Sam, who finished by adding, 'The only thing missing today is my mother. I wish she was here to share in our happiness, and hope she is watching over us. I just know she would approve of my beautiful wife Kate.'

I, by this stage, didn't dare look at Jim, continuing to look straight ahead, hoping no one would notice my embarrassment, sat in what should have been her rightful place. Jim squeezed my hand under the long white cloth covering the table and a multitude of other sins. I knew then he needed me here, as much as I needed him, and placed my hand in his before raising a glass to Kate and Sam's mother, then onto a lighter note from the best man.

The formalities over, the bride and groom disappeared once more for a few more photos before the sun finally set on a beautiful day. They joined us again, now able to relax a little more with drinks and friends, before everyone left for afternoon tea at Kate's parents' house, and an opportunity to say farewell to the newly married couple before they left for their honeymoon; the first couple of nights staying in a luxury country house hotel not too far from home, then onto a friends remote holiday cottage, enjoying an enviable position, perched right above a secluded beach, again not too far away, having only a week, never needing to go far to enjoy breathtaking scenery and seclusion.

The drive to Kate's house was as every bit impressive as the arrival to the hotel, a long sweeping driveway between beautifully manicured lawns, leading you to a most impressive country house, making mine almost insignificant in comparison. We were greeted in the large entrance hall, beautifully lit by a large crystal chandelier, by butlers taking our coats, then waiters offering us flutes, filled with more bubbling Champagne, sat on polished silver trays, explaining as we took one that we were to join the other guests in the drawing room, this time lit by warm standard and table lamps, with the addition of tall candles standing either side of the mantel in polished silver sticks, flickering above the roaring fire, set in a cast iron fireplace, minimalist, compared to mine covered in photos. Here, their portraits were displayed on the walls in oils, depicting their family history, and no doubt the age of the property. Other than that, there was what looked like a very valuable sculpture in the form of a hare sat on the windowsill, looking quite at home within the context of the room, but maybe not with the period of the house.

Kate's parents had now arrived and were mingling with the other guests, none of whom choosing to sit on the richly upholstered sofas and chairs dotted around the room. Although warm, the room was a little impersonal, never the less, a perfect space for entertaining and impressing your guests', whilst your staff addressed their every need. A waiter arrived by our sides with slate platters filled with savoury canapés, followed by another with more Champagne, or the option of a non-alcoholic sparkling wine, which Jim continued to choose to drink, the waiter explaining tea and coffee were also available in the orangery across the hallway; which I just had to explore, as well as an excuse to escape Kate's mother's wandering eye. The grandeur continued into another beautiful room with magnificent views out to the garden and beyond. The tables were laid with not only tea and coffee pots and fine china, but also bite-sized sandwiches and cakes, presented on tired cake stands alongside a pile of tiny white linen serviettes, they had thought of everything. Kate's mother, seemingly quite comfortable for the staff to wander through her house, just as they seemed in it, giving the impression it wasn't the first time they had worked here; I imagine they would be present at any drinks or dinner party held in this household, and expect there will be a stunning dining room somewhere else in the house to host these grand occasions.

'Have you ever been here before?' I ask Jim.

'Once or twice. Drinks at Christmas, that sort of thing.'

'I bet that's a wonderful event in this house,' I remark. 'Jim, I know you're busy next week with the cows, but I'm going to be away,' I explain.

'But I was going to introduce you to them, had you forgotten?'

'No, not at all.' *How could I have forgotten that!* I thought to myself. 'I can still come, it will just have to be Monday, if that's all right. I need to attend a funeral.'

'Oh, I'm sorry,' Jim apologises. 'Is it someone close?'

'That's where it gets complicated,' I explain. 'It's a long story, and here's not the place to start telling you.'

At which point a waiter arrives to explain we are to make our way back to the entrance hall, as the bride and groom are about to depart.

Once Kate and Sam had left, showered again in more confetti before being whisked away in a chauffeur driven car; something else I expect may also be a regular occurrence around here, Jim suggests he takes me home, saying, 'I'll see to the cows with Harry and then I'll come back, and we can talk.'

After Jim had left, I changed into something more comfortable and switched on the television, not needing to eat or drink any more till tomorrow. It didn't seem long before Jim arrived back, despite having had to change, shower and dress again, still omitting his comforting aroma as he sat down beside me.

'So, what's so complicated?' he asks, making himself comfortable.

'I don't really know where to start,' I say.

'At the beginning!' Jim suggests.

'That's such a long time ago now,' I begin.

'Well, whose funeral is it?' Jim enquires.

'Frank's father's.'

'So why is that so difficult?' Jim asks.

'That's where it gets difficult,' I continue. 'Frank was adopted as a baby, before our parents knew each other, and before I was born. Then, my mother met Frank's father through work, and from what I can gather they must have had a brief affair, resulting in me! I've only found this out since my mother's death. My father had asked for my help to sort through all my mother's things. He hadn't wanted to keep any of her clothes; he'd said he'd got photos of her wearing most things that had special connections, and a house full of things she'd collected to make their home. He asked me to take a box away to sort through, he said he'd had a quick look and realised it contained all the things she'd kept from when I was young, for when they next had another baby, which of course never happened, and then I never had one of my own, so it'd just remained unopened all these years later. Instead of just putting it away, curiosity had got the better of me and I had looked inside. On the top were my first shoes, a book of nursery rhymes, my bear and Rose, my baby doll. I'd continued rummaging, until I reached what I'd thought to be the bottom, but wrapped in a pram blanket was a five-year diary,' I pause, recalling my excitement. 'I'd opened it up, unprepared for what I was about to discover. There where periods of blank pages, and the usual dates to remember, as you'd expect, before I'd found my birthday, each year underneath the other. One year read: I looked more like Phil than his own son, or so she thought.'

'Are you sure you aren't misinterpreting what was written?' Jim asks. 'Babies don't always look like their parents.'

'No, there was more; apparently, I have his "misty blue eyes and black wavy hair" that no one only she noticed. My parents were both blonde!'

'Come here,' Jim says, wrapping me in his arms to console me. 'The fact your father hadn't noticed must have meant he had no reason to suspect otherwise, that he accepted and loved you without question. Whatever had happened was over, maybe before it had really started by the sound of things.'

'The sad thing is, that my mother always discouraged my friendship with Frank, with no explanation. We still continued seeing each other, but behind her back. She must have worried I would become fond, even fall in love with who she thought to be my brother, unable to explain her concerns without my father finding out.'

'So, do you think Frank's father had known?' Jim asks.

'It seems not, just my mother, then myself, and of course Frank.'

'So, you never told either of your fathers?' Jim considers.

'No, we decided there was no need to upset anyone else with our findings.'

'And you're sure your father doesn't know, had never found the diary?'

'Absolutely,' I say, with certainty.

'So you have kept it to yourself all this time?'

'Yes, and I will take her secret to the grave with me. I can trust you not to say anything, even to Sarah?' I ask Jim, having only ever spoken to Frank about it.

'Of course you can! I think you must already realise that by now. Your secret is safe with me. What a shame your mother and father never had a baby of their own.'

'That's the thing, I gather from reading the diary, that my mother concluded my father must have been infertile,' I sigh. 'If it hadn't been for Frank's father, I wouldn't be here.'

'Things often have a way of happening for a reason,' Jim concludes.

'I think so too,' I add, 'but I'm still finding it difficult to accept, so much has changed in such a short space of time. Perhaps going back will help.'

'I hope so,' says Jim. 'When is the funeral?'

'Wednesday, but I will travel up on Tuesday. I've booked into a local hotel for a couple of nights. I've been summoned to meet with the solicitor on Thursday morning.'

'I wish I could come with you, but you know I can't leave Harry on his own. It's an impossible task for one person on his own. I can't even stay with you tonight.' Then suddenly, Jim asks, 'Why don't you come back with me now, pack a bag, I want to be with you tonight.'

'I don't know, it's been a long day, and I've still things to get ready for going away,' I say. 'You need to sleep, you're up early. Let's leave it.'

'As long as you're sure. I do love you,' he assures me.

'I'm glad about that, because I love you. Thank you for listening.'

Chapter 9
Back to Our Roots

Jim arrived, still quite early in the morning, not needing to remind me to pick up my wellies on the way out. When Jim had first mentioned the idea of meeting his special herd, I had felt more trepidation than the usual nerves associated with meeting family and friends, which is how Jim referred to them, each cow having a name and personality, they were his pride and joy. I hadn't yet disclosed my fear of the beasts, always choosing to take the long route when out walking, rather than trudge towards these animals, unsure of how they might react, especially after seeing how fast they can run! But just recently, I'd had too much else on my mind to think about that. The farmhouse wasn't what I'd envisaged, never having stumbled across it, despite it being so close to home; hidden from the road, tucked away in a valley down a long track amongst open countryside; birds darting deep into the hedgerows. I couldn't yet see the cows, but could hear they had obviously sensed our arrival.

After a tour of the house, not at all what I'd imagined when forming an impression of two men living on a farm, in fact quite the contrary. The kitchen was traditional, but large and modern, with lots of cupboard space to store things out of the way, leaving the surfaces uncluttered. In addition, there was a large boot room for them to kick off their wellies, hang up their overalls and wash, before crossing the corridor into the kitchen, which then became the dining room; not unlike Sarah's, until you reached the large glass doors that led outside and onto a magnificent terrace and uninterrupted view. The formal entrance was at the front of the house, between two reception rooms, one Jim's, the other belonging to Sam and Kate, allowing each their own privacy, and opportunity to fall asleep in front of whatever programme they chose. The moment I'd been dreading arrived!

Jim, unable to contain his excitement any longer! I donned my jacket and wellies, almost like a surfer preparing to ride the waves, which at this moment seemed a far more attractive proposition! Jim led me out through the boot room into the yard and away from the comfort of the house, till we reached a gate that led us into the meadow where his beloved creatures were supposedly grazing. Jim, seemingly able to recognise each cow before we even got close, introducing each as we wandered.

'Gertie, just here,' Jim greets her like he's greeting a dog, 'is very well behaved. She's got a good temperament and produces a very respectable amount of milk.'

'As long as she's on her best behaviour today,' I comment. 'Aren't they all as well behaved as Gertie?'

'Flora is a little bossy. She likes to show the others she's boss and makes sure she's always first in for milking. Pancake, over there, is another who likes to be first in the parlour for milking; been producing milk for nearly twelve years now, and one of the best.'

'So how old is your oldest?' I ask, now hooked.

'Gertie's the oldest, she's fifteen. But the oldest we've had was twenty. She'd had fifteen calves.'

'So, have you still got her calves?' I ask, looking around, realising they would no longer look like calves, as well as the fact I wouldn't recognise them, although I had noticed that each cow did in fact have different markings, something I hadn't noticed before.

'Yes, Tulip, she's one of my favourite, a lot like her mother, and Primrose over there, though she seems to prefer her own company, goes wandering off on her own, and always has dirty legs!'

We eventually turn and head back the way we had come to the safety of the house, where Jim had promised to make me lunch.

***

I hadn't enjoyed the journey north on my own; Jim had been mortified that he was unable to accompany me, it had just been unfortunate timing, one of those things that can't be helped. There was nothing either of us could do to change things. I would have appreciated his company, but would have perhaps found it difficult once there, still believing it belonged to just Frank and I; still not wanting, or ready to share it with Jim, or if I'm honest, anyone else, especially when I have other things to contend with.

The funeral now thankfully over, I'm now faced with the news received this morning, from the solicitor. Sophie, myself, and Frank's daughter Grace, had each been mentioned in Frank's father's will, as well as leaving us individual possessions and a letter, he had bequeathed the sum from the sale of his house to be split between us, which I had not been expecting.

My letter had ended: *'Our dear Molly, take your time enjoying it once more, I know how special it was to you. Take from it what you will, but share your stories with Grace, so she remembers her dad.*

Take care of yourself my dear. We loved you like our own, you were the daughter we never had.

God bless dearest Molly.'

Frank's daughter, Grace, had had to leave, Sophie suggesting I visit the house on my own first, to be alone with my own thoughts, but to call her when I was ready, and she would make us something to eat. I entered through the front door, despite having seen Phil in recent years, I had never actually visited here since a child. Sophie had obviously been in and tidied since Phil had been in hospital, ready for his return. Everything was where it belonged, even fresh logs in the basket beside the fire in the living room. The same crotched cushion that Frank's mother had made was plumped in the back of an armchair, waiting to be sat in. The house was cold, being November, perhaps Sophie and I would come in together tomorrow and light a fire whilst we sorted through some things together. The cracked wobbly tile on the floor as I entered the kitchen still hadn't been repaired, and the freestanding oven that Alice had so often stood in front of, had been replaced for a more modern built-in version, along with different cupboard fronts than the ones I remember, the contents though remained the same: empty jars waiting to be filled with summer fruits, the large glass jug, so often filled with elderflower cordial, cake tins, always bursting with beautifully decorated treats and empty flasks waiting to be filled and taken out on an adventure. Being presented with the box my father had given me had been difficult enough, but bore no resemblance to opening the door on my childhood, sadly, without Frank and his mother to share it. There was still the pine plate rack displaying pretty dinner plates and teacups hanging below, and the old table under the window where Frank and I had so often shared a sandwich and drink. I turned and familiarised myself with upstairs, having only ever visited the bathroom, whose handle still didn't latch! I answered my phone, Jim had tried calling earlier whilst I was in the solicitor's office and I'd forgotten to call him back. I sit down on the plump eiderdown, covering what had once been Frank's bed, spilling my heart out to him, explaining how I can't come home yet, having been unprepared for the news I'd just received. Jim sharing my mood, feeling useless, being unable to join me.

'I've got Sophie,' I tell Jim, as much to reassure him as well as myself.

'But she must be as upset as you are. Whereas I haven't got that emotional attachment,' Jim explains. 'Call me if you need me, whenever, it's the least I can do until Sam returns, and then I'll be straight up to join you. I love you Molly.'

Needing some fresh air, I head out into the back garden, the sun now low in the sky, I sit on the old wooden bench, still in the same position under the apple tree, now stripped of life like the house behind me. I open the gate at the bottom of the garden that leads directly onto the riverbank, where Frank and I had been free to roam and forage, more like Ratty and Mole than the intrepid Secret Seven, braving nettles and thorns each autumn, getting prickled and purple, reaching for the juiciest berries. Without realising, I was already under the sweet chestnut tree, stamping on the prickly shells just as Frank and I had learnt to do to retrieve the nuts to roast, always discarding the smaller ones for the squirrels. The light was fading as I turned back towards Sophie's house, as I had as a child needing protection and warmth. Tomorrow we would help each other to come to terms with what was left.

A new day dawned with a covering of frost, and the leaves now falling in quick succession from the oak tree across the road. Both Sophie and I had been unable to sleep, contemplating the day ahead, so had made an early start on an unpredictable day. It appeared Phil had been a very organised person, and had prepared for the inevitable eventuality, relieving us of hours of sorting through documents. In one of the bedrooms he had labelled boxes, with their contents and the recipient's name. It appeared he had still been in possession of many of Frank's things, including trophies, his scout handbook, drumsticks, model aeroplanes, his collection of music—then published on vinyl, all now accounting for the apparent lack of accumulated material that had followed Frank into our house. More to the point—what do I do with it all now! There were several boxes containing photo albums from the moment Frank was born, depicting everything from his first steps to him leaving home. These days, all these moments are stored somewhere in a cloud, more than likely remaining unopened. But, when Sophie and I take a break, we carry some of the albums downstairs with us to share with a cup of tea and another box. Inside is his stamp collection, does anyone even send letters anymore? And a diary, which I suppose is the equivalent of sharing your movements on Facebook. Was I expected to keep all this stuff, perhaps Grace may be interested in reading about, how on July 29th her father tried his first cigarette, whilst she's listening to "Pink Floyd" on YouTube!

After much laughing and crying, Sophie and I decided we'd done all we could for now, locking the door on our tears and happiness, taking away the memories that remained, realising I didn't need to be here to keep them alive, that they would always be with me wherever I went. Frank and I had made new memories together, which is where I belonged now, even without Frank there.

I went to bed happier than I had felt in a long while, having spent the day with Sophie helping me make sense of all the irregularities in life, and realising just how much I missed Jim, and how much I was looking forward to seeing him when I stepped off the train tomorrow. I had called him earlier explaining I'd made the decision to return home, unable, either physically or emotionally to do anything else for the time being.

Chapter 10
Advent

A new day dawned as Jim and I strolled down to the church to join Sarah and the rest of the family for the service as usual. It felt like so much had happened since this time last Sunday; at the same time, realising I was now ready to make new memories with Jim and his family.

Unlike the city, the first signs of Christmas in our little coastal village were the tiny lanterns glowing in the windows of the Smugglers Inn on the top of the hill, their door now firmly shut with a substantial wreath made from holly, fir, berries and dried oranges, hanging from below the knocker. The children were always the first to get into the spirit of things, displaying garlands of coloured tinsel and paper chains from inside their old school windows, normally lit in the fading light of December afternoons, keeping their spirits high, if that was necessary! Further down the road, the bakery, closed today, will fill its window with warm mince pies, decorated with stars and sprinkled with icing sugar, and gingerbread men with currants for eyes, hanging behind the little panes of glass, and of course a selection of now beautifully decorated Christmas cakes.

We reach the church much earlier than I would have, if left to my own devices, unlatching the heavy oak door releasing the fragrance of fresh Chrysanthemums and candles, shutting it behind us to keep in the warmth. The service starts with the lighting of the first candle on the Advent wreath, a symbol of hope and eternity, before singing Hymn number 38, a familiar reminder of Christmas for me.

Despite the sun shining, it is still cold as we step out from the warmth of the church. I am tempted to walk round the side of the church to be close to Frank, but feel it would be inappropriate in the presence of Jim and his family. I will return tomorrow when I can be alone.

'Come on Molly,' Jim calls.

I turn and follow him out of the gate and up the road towards Sarah's.

'Let's get warm inside and you can tell us all about your trip,' Sarah says, as we pile in through the door, festooned with holly and fairy lights; all eager to stand in front of the now ebbing flames that are left of the fire.

'Let me get that going,' Jim says, as we filter through into the kitchen, now transformed for the festive season, Hyacinth bulbs sit on top of jars, and the windowsill above the sink is dotted with candles, above which, is another string of lights. The meat, having been left to roast in the oven, is now omitting a wonderful aroma, and the vegetables, as usual, have all been prepared and the wine opened, all that is left to do is put the pans onto boil.

'Let me help,' I suggest to Sarah, taking the cutlery from her.

'I bet you're glad you can put the last week behind you and enjoy Christmas,' she begins.

'Yes,' I reply, 'it was difficult, but necessary, as funerals inevitably are.'

'But what was it like going back?' Sarah continues.

'Helpful,' I admit. 'It helped me put things into perspective.'

'Dad was worried you might decide to stay, relieved when you said you were coming back.'

'It had crossed my mind, but like I said, it helped me put things into perspective, and besides, I haven't forgotten I'm looking after Luke and Lizzie after Christmas,' I remind her.

'Is the wine open?' Jim asks eagerly, as he enters the room.

'I've only opened one today,' says Sarah. 'Sam and Kate aren't coming. I think they must still be in honeymoon mode!'

'Have you spoken to them yet?' I ask.

'Only briefly,' Sarah says, glancing towards Jim. I guess looking for a reaction, Jim having stayed over at mine last night. But I don't think he registers her curiosity, showing no embarrassment; I have come to realise men are oblivious to subtle innuendoes!

After enjoying a few brace of pheasants, shot earlier this week by a friend of Jim's, we relax in front of the fire whilst the children, whose appetite now satisfied, play contentedly together with brief interactions from the adults. The foliage doesn't yet extend to this room, where I imagine a tree, impinging on the floor space used by Luke and Lizzie to spread themselves out with their toys. Although mine won't be going up just yet either, preferring everything else to be in order before hanging chocolate snowmen and Santas wrapped in brightly coloured foil from drooping branches for any excited visitors, of which I have many.

As if reading my thoughts, Luke jumps up, 'Mummy, we haven't opened our Advent calendars today.'

'You're right, do you want to go and get them?'

Lizzie, realising what Luke has remembered, stops what she is doing to follow him and retrieve her own calendar.

'Help me find mine, Luke,' she demands.

I consider how lucky she is to have a big brother to look out for her, imagining them growing even closer in years to come; a love that will endure all that life entails.

Jim and I appear inseparable, making the most of Sam's return, and before I know it, another week has passed; Megan is lighting the second candle on the Advent wreath and Luke is opening the thirteenth window on his calendar. Only twelve days left, and I still haven't bought, let alone written any cards! Jim proving too much of a distraction, was instructed to return home for a brief spell, which in total amounted to ten hours, returning just as I had written the address on my last card. All I had to do now was buy and wrap the remaining presents, and of course buy and decorate the tree. Thankfully, Sarah was taking care of the catering, though I would be contributing bottles and bakes and the obligatory chocolate liquors, an absolute must, that I have introduced into many households over the years.

'Am I welcome?' Jim asks me, as he wanders into the kitchen freshly showered. How could I say no!

'Looks like you might need help hanging these, I don't think there's any space left on the windowsills,' he says, as he hands me a pile of cards he's picked up from the doormat.

It's true, every available space had been filled. I have accumulated many friends over the years, some, admittedly, I only hear from each Christmas, but would miss if I didn't. I begin opening the white envelopes. On top of the pile, as I'd guessed, is a card from Daisy; each year continuing to support the same charity, ever since she discovered her little black velvet dress hanging in her high-street shop window. Since then she has never looked back, donating anything and everything, from her bras to her wedding dress, in an attempt to transform lives. Inside, she's written a short note explaining how this year, she'd asked the children at school, to instead of writing each other a Christmas card, to put the money towards buying an Oxfam goat, already having enough donated to purchase two! I myself, choose cards from the RNLI each year, appreciating the conditions they have to endure to save lives, as well as the obligatory pack to support Daisy, making an exception in her case, having enclosed a ten-pound note to add to her donation rather than a gift, knowing which she would prefer. The next card I open, is hand illustrated. James, who I had once looked after, now grown up and an illustrator for children's books, had taken the time to sketch a melting snowman. I imagine no two cards ever the same, practicing his thoughts and ideas, just as he had always enjoyed as a child. Beth, his sister, has also sent a lovely card, this year with the addition of Joshua, her son's name, born earlier this year. She has also included a photo of him in her mother's arms, and a short note that sums up her pride and joy at becoming a mother. I so enjoy receiving more than 'love and best wishes' inside an envelope, it is such a shame that emails and messaging have almost eliminated the art of letter writing; there is something quite romantic about communicating in the way generations before us once did. Computers and smart phones may be more efficient, but they can never replace that kind of sentimental history. I open one more, before going to relax in front of the fire I'd made earlier in the living room.

'Isn't this beautiful?' I say, showing Jim the card I have just pulled from its envelope, 'I do love a bit of glitter!' Jenny's card is, as always, covered in the obligatory glitter, knowing just how much I loved any excuse to get it out, we would find it in everything, weeks into January! I still love its magic and sparkle.

'I can see you're going to have fun with the children after Christmas,' Jim says. 'I forgot to mention, Sarah's invited us to Luke's nativity play at school next week. You will accompany me, won't you?' he asks.

'I'd love too,' I reply. 'I've so missed the children's school nativity performances since finishing my last appointment and moving here.'

'We're in for a real treat by all accounts. Luke has been cast as an angel.'

'Perhaps we could invite Sarah and Henry here one evening before Christmas, if Sam and Kate would look after the children,' I suggest. 'Sarah's always cooking.'

'She'd like that, I'm sure. Let me know a date and I'll tell her,' Jim replies.

'How about Friday? There's a Christmas market on down at the quay later this week. We could buy a tree and decorate it together,' I suggest. 'Have you finished all your Christmas shopping?'

'Nearly,' Jim replies. 'You?'

'Same,' I sigh.

'How about we go away this weekend?' Jim suggests. 'Explore, finish our shopping, and enjoy the festivities.'

'Lets!' I agree.

Somehow Jim and I found time to buy a tree and decorate, not only this, but the whole house in anticipation of Sarah and Henry's arrival. Clusters of jars twinkled with candle light, and fresh holly adorned the fireplace. Jim had got his wish, receiving a kiss under the mistletoe he had hung in the hallway, leaving the berries intact, refusing to comply with tradition and spoil his fun! We had enjoyed a lovely evening together, dining on a traditional lamb tagine, that had filled the house with its Moroccan spices for several hours, accompanied by a Goose IPA, the perfect balance of citrus, spice and herbs, discovered at the market. I served the beer in large wine goblets rather than the usual pint-sized straight glasses, not just so I could pick it up, or even for aesthetic purposes, but, like a good wine, to appreciate the rich aromas and taste. For dessert, I'd prepared a sticky toffee pudding, layered with dates left over from the tagine, matching this with a dark beer, with a heady, stewed fruit aroma, perfect for a heavy dessert such as this. Then to finish, a pot of Jin Zhan Mo Li, Marigold tea, perfect after a heavy meal, and caffeine free. The pot I'd chosen was glass, usually used for my herbs, but was perfect to appreciate the beautiful golden marigold and jasmine flowers unfurl, like a sea anemone. It had been such a lovely evening spent together, so nice to see Sarah relax for a change, making a mental note to do this more often.

Our weekend away had been both luxurious and magical. It had been nice to escape and enjoy each other's company away from home, if only for a brief spell. Jim had spared no expense and had booked us into a small boutique hotel overlooking the quayside, about an hour from home. The balcony doors at the foot of the bed overlooked the river, a lot busier stretch than I had known as a child. Jim had ordered breakfast in bed so we could enjoy the view. The food was exceptional and there was even a double bath for us to relax in together. We did however manage to escape these luxuries for a while, meandering through the bustling streets along with other couples and families out shopping for gifts, or just feasting on the festive atmosphere, everywhere decorated for Christmas, even the little shop windows aglow in the fading light. Further along the quayside a brass band was playing carols, their poor fingers must have been freezing, probably welcoming a march up the high street today, but instead just stamped their feet between the music. We had found a little bookshop and chosen a couple of Christmas stories for the children, I adore these little shops that still exist, always choosing to support them rather than buy online. So many small independent shops we once took for granted are now few and far between. Although recently, I was still able to buy a few balls of wool for less than ten pounds, to knit a pair off bootees, gloves, and a hat for a present for a newborn baby, after discovering a gift set including the same three items for almost a hundred pounds in a high-street shop! These items obviously still in demand, but harder to find, the art of which diminishing, along with baking and sewing, each of which now having popular programmes on television, with huge viewing figures, demonstrating simple skills that I was taught as a child, but now considered a talent rather than an everyday task. Perhaps it won't be long before there's a knitting channel, demonstrating different stiches and patterns. Even bakeries, providing an everyday staple have declined as more supermarkets are built. People choosing the convenience of picking up a loaf with the rest of their groceries and prepared to pay astronomical amounts for both cupcakes and macaroons, when the actual cost, time and skill required is minimal. Fortunately, we have retained ours, it being a long journey to the nearest supermarket. Instead of freezing more than I need, I always have the ingredients to bake some sort of loaf, something I enjoy doing, especially over Christmas.

The countdown had now begun. The children's interpretation of the nativity had been a huge success and very entertaining, knowing from experience, that no matter how well rehearsed it appears, there was no telling how the children would behave on the day, left to their own devices!

As ever, everyone is preparing frantically as the day draws nearer. I join the crowds in a nearby town, queuing for more wrapping paper, having miscalculated in my estimation. On returning to the car, my attention is drawn, not to the window of the charity shop on the corner, which despite the array of items they get donated, are still unable to create the same stunning and imaginative displays that adorn Oxford Street during the festive season. If only those window dressers would donate their time to wave their magic hands over these unloved garments and paraphernalia to transform and add sparkle to them once again. Instead my attention is drawn to the car parked outside with its engine still running and boot open. The shop, more popular than any of the others in the town, either because the people here love animals more than supporting lives at sea, or transforming lives in the developing world, or it's the fact that cars can park directly outside and offload their unwanted belongings. Customers often drawn in, as Daisy was, by a garment in a window for their own personal gain, rather than that of the charity. There haven't always been as many charity shops as there are now, items previously handed down, or kept and used again, other items repaired rather than replaced, only occasionally donating something, to make room for something else—often to the White Elephant stall at the church fete, where I remember finding four of the prettiest little cake plates, decorated with a delicate pink-floral design and edged in gold. One year as a child, I had bought a small game in a cloth bag, once home and on closer inspection, I had found a love letter tucked inside along with the instructions, left wondering, if Catherine had ever received, or was possibly still looking for it! The chances of finding a letter today greatly diminished along with the sacred art of letter writing. I also remember collecting silver milk-bottle tops to send to Blue Peter to help buy a guide dog for the blind, reminding me to give my coloured plastic-bottle tops to Luke to take to school, adding to their collection for prosthetic limbs.

Once home I pick up the post, dropping it on the kitchen table before filling the kettle. Despite enjoying Jim's company, I do still cherish time to myself occasionally, as I had before Frank died, perhaps having been on my own for so long before. I take the assorted envelopes and small package through to the warmth of the living room where I can relax and enjoy my coffee whilst opening them, choosing the package first. Inside, is a letter from Sophie, explaining the contents of the package: a photo of Frank sat under a Christmas tree when he was a young child. Also included, is a little parcel wrapped in white tissue paper. Inside, is a beautiful six-pointed gold star, sprinkled with gold glitter and threaded with gold string, which Sophie had found whilst sorting through a box of Alice's treasures. Frank and I had always disagreed as to what should sit on top of the Christmas tree, agreeing to disagree, deciding instead to alternate what would sit there. One year an angel, the following year, Frank would adorn the top with a star. I immediately take off the star that has adorned the Christmas tree ever since Frank was first diagnosed, granting him this wish, replacing it with the glittering gold one. Sophie's letter continues with news of someone already interested in Frank's house, a young couple looking for their first home together in the village, having heard through the grapevine of its vacant possession, and not wanting to lose out on the opportunity of acquiring it, would be willing to pay the full market value to secure it, understanding the circumstances and prepared to wait until we are ready to proceed. Sophie continuing to explain that they are already living with the young woman's mother, so had no property of their own to sell.

Taking advantage of Jim enjoying a day at the farm, and now that I've replenished the wrapping paper, I decide to wrap up the remaining presents, including a bottle of cologne for Jim, having noticed the bottle in his bathroom was dwindling, and enjoying every precious drop of this provocative mix of spices, I had continued to add hair and body shampoo and shave balm to my basket to intensify the fragrance and penetrate deep into his pores, satisfying my own guilty pleasure. Disguised in a gift bag, I place them under the tree along with the other presents, noticing how many more there are this year, realising just how quickly things have changed, becoming part of Jim's family. Suddenly missing Frank and realising I hadn't visited him for a while, not that he was ever far from my thoughts, I pull on my coat and boots and head out into the sunshine. I call in at Lyndsey's shop and pick a few assorted blooms, including four red roses to add to the mix, realising that they would most probably not survive long outside, but remembering my promise to always remember him and bring him fresh flowers. I sit and talk to him, remembering happier times of our first Christmas here together, when it had even snowed. We'd been so excited, we'd rushed outside before opening any of our presents to build a snowman, able to use a carrot for his nose from the bag to be peeled for our Christmas lunch. It seems so long ago now, despite only having two Christmases together here. I hope I will never forget the sound of his sweet voice or his warm embrace, this time he was gone for ever, our paths would never cross again.

Jim and I woke up beside each other in the bed we now shared in Honeysuckle cottage, preferring to contain our excitement and conserve our energy for the remainder of what promised to be an eventful Christmas day, rather than accept Sarah's kind offer to stay over last night. As always, we joined them in church, today lighting the remaining candle on the Advent wreath, reminding us of Christ's love, and to sing the now well-rehearsed carols we were all now familiar with. The children gathered to see baby Jesus now lying in the manger, having arrived last night along with the shepherds and animals. The service was relatively short, perhaps James had already conducted the midnight service, or was just keen to get away to enjoy his lunch! We concluded the service by singing "We Three Kings" whilst one of the altar boys processed between the isles swinging the gold thurible with gay abandon, releasing the fragrant smoke, reminding us of the gifts brought from afar, although Melchior, Gaspar and Balthazar were still nowhere to be seen, unless of course you'd spotted them on the windowsill at the back of the church!

Lizzie carried her new baby doll home carefully, saying, 'I'm going to call my baby, Jesus.'

Luke enquiring, 'Can she do that Mummy?'

'Well he is a baby boy, and he did arrive on Christmas morning,' Sarah replies.

We step through Sarah's front door, releasing the delicious smell of the turkey cooking away. Henry orders Jim and I into the kitchen to join himself and Sarah in a toast to a happy Christmas with a glass of Champagne, topped with sparkling pomegranate seeds to add to the festive spirit. For a moment, I remember raising a glass with Frank, but without the pomegranate seeds, or a thought to a future without him. I raise my glass, as I had a prayer with the clouds of fragrant smoke ascending to Heaven.

Chapter 11
New Beginnings

The carol singers had sung and hung up their lanterns for another year. The cards had come down, and the Christmas tree had been taken outside until we remembered what to do with it. Frank's star had been placed carefully within the box of decorations before going back into the loft for another year. The remaining chocolate Santas now sat in a small bowl in the kitchen, though I expect, not for long! The socks, chocolates and toiletries that had lived under the tree for so long, had now been put in their rightful places, and the empty bottles were out at the front awaiting collection. Jim and I were on our way to take Luke to school and Lizzie to nursery, collecting her again at lunch time before Sarah arrived home. My new year's resolution had been renewed, and as yet, I was doing well, despite it being my first day, having left the house in good time. Each year I resolved to be more organised, whether Jim's punctuality would have the desired effect, would remain to be seen! I think I had developed my bad habits, not from my own parents, whose precision in time keeping was exemplary, but from Sophie, who was late for everything! I always seemed to arrive at school just as the bell was rung in the playground, or once the Brownies had lined up together in their Six. No wonder I never got to be a Sixer! Even now my birthday card from her arrives late. Though, despite her faults, she has a heart of gold and taught me all I know, or most of it. She had persevered until I was able to tie my own laces on my new black patent ankle boots, and then the ribbons on my ballet shoes. Had set me handwriting exercises, first with a pencil and then with a fountain pen, eager to copy her beautiful scrolls. Then as I got older, to knit, although she never quite knew how to pick up a dropped stitch, resulting in either taking it all back to the beginning, or living with a hole in your work! Alice had introduced me to nature's kitchen, and Frank and I had discovered the outdoors and all its wonders, that lay just beyond the garden gate.

Once we'd delivered the children to school and nursery, the rest of the morning was ours until collecting Lizzie at lunchtime. The demands on my time had been greater, back in the day, but not so distant past, when I had sole responsibility for the children in my care, whose parents sometimes didn't arrive home until after their babies were tucked up in bed where they had left them. Each time I would fall hopelessly in love, with each and every one of them, especially, if like their mother I'd cradled them from birth, shared their sleepless nights, their sadness and their joy, sat through countless school performances and stood on the touch line in the freezing cold, whilst Matthew discovered he was never going to achieve his dream and play for England in the world cup.

As the children grew so had my desire for a new family with a new baby, never considering it may just have been my own body clock ticking. Perhaps it was this that had prevented me from falling in love with an eligible man and starting a family of our own. Now obviously too late, time waits for no man, and the window of opportunity had passed. But still, regardless of this, I have gained so many happy memories that I'll cherish forever. It may have taken a long time, but Frank and I had found love in the end. Even Luke and Lizzie have started calling me Grandma. Luke having corrected himself on Christmas day, beginning with 'Grandma'. Then Lizzie had found it amusing, repeating it. Sarah had mentioned to them, that I might just like to be called Grandma. Now it just rolls off their tongues. Even Jim, after repeating it several times, has now got used to it, making me feel loved and very special.

Another perk of Sarah being a teacher, is that she is able to look after the children during the school holidays, leaving us to do whatever we please, and now that it's the February half term we are on our way to celebrate a very romantic Valentine's day with Jim's oldest and best friend Bob, who is about to get married to his fiancée Linda. Bob, also the local postman had met Linda, the school secretary, in the same school he had attended with his first wife. Bob, had in fact married his childhood sweetheart the first-time round, eventually growing apart, losing the passion they'd once shared, discovering the more they knew one another, the less they liked each other. Whereas Frank and I had spread our wings before finally settling down together. Our relationship had been one of best friends playing out together: discovery and adventure. It wouldn't have felt right sitting together on the back row in the cinema, or kissing under the tree outside the gate at the bottom of the garden. We were too busy exploring new boundaries, making new memories of our own to stop for a moment and consider each other.

Jim, provided a brief history of Bob's family in the car on our way to the wedding. As far as he could remember, his son was still living and working in London during the week, one of many, accounting for the highest population of second homes in England. Not that Mrs Gilbert, living at Gull cottage would agree, having lived here all her life, not taking kindly to Frank and myself, or any of the second home owners on her own doorstep, worried one day she won't recognise her own neighbours and the village becoming a ghost town in the winter. The fact is, there are more families leaving because there are more opportunities open to them these days. Places have changed not only here, but up and down the country; families and communities once built around the industrial revolution having disappeared, along with their annual two weeks' holiday, when the mines and the mills would shut down and the workers and their families would all board the train together and set off to their local coastal town. These too, having changed in character, from deckchairs on the beach to party revellers attending hen do's and stag parties. More people now prepared to travel further afield, more often abroad, a percentage owning holiday homes there. Despite these changes, local traditions are still retained: brass bands formed by the colliery workers, still exist and thrive, as do fishermen singing their shanties. We may not have pilchards, but fresh crabs and lobsters are landed here each day. I'm sure if Mrs Gilbert had her wish, we'd still be eating stargazy pie, and there'd be pirates in the caves of the hidden coves!

Bob's daughter had remained closer to home, whilst her husband, in Mrs Gilberts eyes, is responsible for selling the properties that come onto the market to whoever can afford to buy them. Some people taking advantage of the huge sums on offer that people are prepared to pay for the chance to own a property in an increasingly popular seaside town, not a million miles from here.

The arrival didn't disappoint, set amidst spectacular woodland was the country manor, all ours, shared with just the bride, groom and the other fifteen guests. Inside was just as stunning, displaying opulent furnishings and lit with beautiful crystal chandeliers hanging from every ceiling, captivating all the magic and charm of a bygone era. Our bedroom didn't disappoint either, beautiful fabric draping the large windows, and even enough space for a roll top bath with a view through the tree tops. The wedding had been planned for later in the day, to be followed by a lavish candle-lit dinner.

With daylight fading, we make our way, creeping quietly into the adjoining barn where the ceremony is to be conducted, beautifully decorated with an abundance of flowers, clusters of candles and a scattering of red rose petals, silence instilled from the moment we step inside. In front of us, I can hear two guys whispering, 'I never expected to be attending my own parents wedding!'

'Better than their funeral though!'

Linda and Bob arrive together, whilst a harpist plays "Thinking out Loud". Linda's long gown is positively elegant, one I may have chosen for myself, reminiscent of the Jane Austin period, draped in fine lace, her veil held under a large floral crown, heavy with crimson and soft orange blooms, entwined within laurel and rosemary, matching her trailing bouquet. Their vows ended, 'Till death do us part'; a love that could last another three decades, longer than their first. Wiser now, than either of them had been when they first made them, with young and fragile hearts, lost in passion. Not that passion doesn't exist at our age, something the younger generation have yet to discover! We follow them out, the harpist continuing to play a selection of beautiful music.

Once back inside the house, we're served saucers of Champagne, whilst the photographer captures a few informal shots of the bride and groom, before leaving them to enjoy the rest of their celebrations without interruption. The table is beautifully set with elegant china, silver cutlery, large candelabras, cut glass and splendour; all reminiscent of a long-lost time, unfortunately, too often forgotten in this day and age. I fear none of these will be going in the dishwasher tonight! The table had groaned with food, fine wine and happiness, before we eventually retired to the drawing room for after dinner drinks, coffee, and good company.

The romance continued through, until the time came to pack up and head off home, listening to the radio, drifting in and out of a gentle slumber as Jim drove.

'Nearly home,' Jim says quietly, giving me a gentle nudge. 'Wakey-wakey!' I open my eyes and spot the wind turbines turning in time to Robbie Williams singing, 'On that famous thoroughfare, with their noses in the air…'

'We had a wonderful time, didn't we?' I say dreamily, already planning a dinner party with the newlyweds, eager to recreate the splendour of last night.

'Wonderful!' Jim agrees.

We'd only been home a matter of moments, when Sophie had called to arrange a date for me to visit before she would inevitably have to hand the keys over from Frank's house, advising me to come prepared as she'd sorted more boxes for my attention. I promised I would call her back once I had spoken to Jim, suggesting it would be a perfect opportunity for them to meet.

The week almost over and another calf had safely arrived into the world, Luke having named the first one, Star, after being awarded star of the week at school for his enthusiasm. Lizzie hadn't had to wait too long for her time, though it had taken a while for her to decide on a name, and after much deliberation arrived at the name Crocus, having just discovered them growing under a tree, explaining to a disagreeable Luke, that her mother Buttercup was named after a flower. Work had been progressing well on the barn conversion and was almost ready for Harry to move in. Jim and I had planned to spoil ourselves again this weekend, taking advantage of an offer for a night away at another country house, but this time closer to the home I had grown up with, somewhere Jim was unfamiliar with, but keen to see for himself, having heard my wonderful memories, that I was now excited to share with him.

The sun was shining, though low in the sky, and the snow drops still out, as we walked together along the riverbank. The water was still, but the otters nowhere to be seen, as I showed Jim where they lived. The birds were visible, darting in and out of the trees, already seemingly busy, despite it not yet spring.

'And you swam in there?' Jim asks, remembering my recollections.

'I learnt to swim in there,' I remind him. 'We'll have to come back in the summer,' I suggest, remembering the fun I'd had.

'And this is Franks house,' I say quietly, almost out of respect, as I twist the handle on the gate and lead Jim into the garden where all my memories had begun. 'This is where I grew up.'

'This is beautiful,' Jim declares, wrapping his arms around me, kissing me gently on the top of my head, 'just as you described it. Thank you for bringing me here.'

'Tomorrow I'll take you inside,' I finish.

The hotel was very charming, with log fires warming each cosy sitting room, the perfect place to relax with your coffee after dinner, before retiring to the sumptuous bed.

I'd woken in the night from a dream, still able to remember Frank standing on our little boat, swaying it from side to side, trying to capsize us, but falling in himself! I had jumped in after him and into his arms. Of course, it had never really happened that way! A wave of sadness washed over me. I wandered over to the window and peered through the curtains, snow was falling, soft, heavy flakes. Without further thought, I jump back in bed to wake Jim.

'Jim, wake up, get dressed!' I demand.

'What's the matter?' he asks, alarmed.

'It's snowing!' I tell him.

'So why do I have to get dressed?' he enquires.

'So we can go and play in it, come on!' I insist. 'We need to build a snowman!'

'Why?' Jim continues. 'Can't we build one in the morning?'

'No,' I tell him, as I pull on my jeans, 'it might all be gone by then!'

Jim, still half asleep, begins to dress in yesterday's clothes.

'Come on, quietly!' I order, as I grab his hand and lead him across the landing.

'Why are we whispering?' Jim asks.

'Because everyone's sleeping!' I remind him.

'Even Luke and Lizzie I expect,' Jim frowns.

I drag him past the empty reception desk and into the porch where there's a selection of wellingtons for the guests use.

'Are we even allowed to go out?' Jim asks me.

'We're guests in a country house,' I remind him. 'Not held at her majesty's pleasure! Now find a pair of boots that're the right size, but don't put them on yet.'

'Why not?' Jim asks, still slightly puzzled.

'Well we can hardly build a snowman in these formal gardens, can we?'

'So where are we going?'

'Follow me,' I explain, 'if we go now, we can be back in time for breakfast.'

'I'm beginning to think you're either mad, or you've simply spent too long in the company of young children. Perhaps you just need to get out more!'

'That's exactly what I'm doing!' I remind him.

After working up an enormous appetite, Jim and I managed to devour a huge breakfast, the waiter quite surprised, after having served us both with five courses the previous evening! The snow as predicted had stopped, but hadn't disappeared, working its magic across the fields and fells.

Sophie appears pleased to see us, especially Jim it seems, greeting him with a warm handshake, 'It's always a pleasure to meet Molly's friends.'

Jim, glancing towards me with a suspicious look on his face, misinterpreting what Sophie had said.

'How are you my dear?' Sophie asks as she wraps her arms around me. 'I hope you've been looking after yourself.'

'I'm just fine,' I assure her, as we sit down in front of the roaring fire, just as I had as a child.

'You'll never guess what I found when I popped round to Frank's this morning to light a fire,' Sophie begins, as she makes her way into the kitchen to put the kettle on.

'I think I can guess!' Jim whispers, looking towards me.

'Shh!' I whisper, as I place a finger to my mouth.

'No, what was it?' I ask, humouring her.

'A snowman!' Sophie informs us.

'Where?' I ask.

'Well, in the back garden, staring at me as I opened the gate. Someone must have crept in quite early,' Sophie deduced, 'because there were no footprints, and it wasn't snowing when I got up at seven.'

'Quite a mystery then,' I add.

'It reminded me of you Miss Molly. You did love the snow, I practically had to drag you in from playing out in it, always afraid it would be gone in the morning,' Sophie reminds me.

'Now why doesn't that surprise me!' Jim mumbles, as he squeezes my waist and follows me into the kitchen.

Sophie had filled us both full of cakes and tea, as she always loved to do, we certainly wouldn't need any lunch today!

'Did you want to take another look in Frank's house?' Sophie enquires. 'It will be the last chance you have. You don't have to, I've brought all the boxes for you to take back with you here.'

'I think I should,' I admit, expecting I would.

'I'll give you the key,' Sophie says, getting up. 'You go before Grace and Lucy get here.'

'Come on Jim, I'd like you to come with me,' I explain.

Once inside, the familiar smells evoke my favourite childhood memories, retained in the thick stone walls. Sophie had obviously been in since we were last here, all that remained were a few pieces of furniture, stripped of their possessions and memories. I now realise, that these are, and always will be, safe, forever in my heart, and as I lock the door behind us, it feels right that someone else will breathe new life and make new memories here.

When we arrived back at Sophie's house, Grace and Lucy had arrived as Sophie had expected. After introducing Jim, we settle down with another cup of tea and start chatting and listening to Lucy's tales of her schooldays, reminding me of Luke.

'I'm looking after a little boy, with Jim, who's your age,' I tell her.

'My, you two are spending a lot of time together!' observes Grace, joining in the conversation, as ever, without thinking first; with whatever she is thinking, written all over her face.

'What's his name, Grandma?' Lucy enquires.

'He's called Luke,' I tell her. 'His name begins with an "L", like your name, and he has a sister called Lizzie.' Leaving it there; that was enough information for Grace to digest for now.

'How old is Lizzie?' Lucy asks. Her little brain catching up, and as inquisitive as her mother.

'Two years old,' I tell her.

'Can I play with them when I come and visit you again?' Lucy asks.

'I'm sure that can be arranged,' I reply.

'Do you want to know what I found in Grandad's garden this morning?' Sophie asks Lucy, changing the subject, perhaps realising where it may lead.

'What Sophie?' Lucy asks, interestedly.

'Shall I keep it a surprise, and show you later?' Sophie suggests.

'I want to know now!' Lucy insists.

'Well if I tell you, I can't show you just yet,' Sophie admits, remembering Lucy's impatience. 'Is that all right?'

'Tell me!' Lucy implores.

'A snowman!' Sophie exclaims.

'Oh, I built one in my garden this morning,' Lucy says, obviously underwhelmed.

I hand the key back to Sophie, before Jim and I head off home in his Land Rover, laden with not only boxes for my attention, but also kitchen equipment, a table lamp and other paraphernalia Sophie thought might be useful for Harry in the new barn conversion, persuading us to take it home with us, saving her a trip to the charity shop, and of course which I'm sure Harry will be grateful for, just as the new couple buying Frank's house were for the remaining furniture, wanting to retain its character as much as possible.

'So, what are we doing next weekend?' Jim asks.

'Funny,' I reply, 'I was just thinking the exact same thing. It was fun, wasn't it?'

'It was wonderful,' Jim smiles. 'I do love you Miss Molly!'

'As I do you,' I reply, closing my eyes.

'Sweet dreams,' Jim whispers as he kisses my hand, and takes me home.

Chapter 12
Contentment and Joy

Jim hadn't quite moved in yet, we still enjoyed our own space, not that we'd grown tired of each other already, but we didn't have the constraints of a young couple with snatched moments together; we could see each other as often as we desired, stay up all night or linger in bed till lunch. Sam had stopped worrying when his father didn't arrive home at night, questioning when he did! Jim admitting, he felt like he had no fixed abode!
This morning I was relaxing in the kitchen, rummaging through the cookery books for inspiration. Whilst away, we had stumbled upon an old bookshop inside a tiny cottage, every wall laden with local history, mainly books, but the odd picture here and there filling in any gaps, much more informative than a local tourist information centre could ever hope to be. A bell had rung as we'd opened the door, awakening an elderly gentleman from his afternoon snooze in a leather arm chair in front of an open fire at the back of the shop. I too, could have quite happily sat in front of that fire each day with a book on my lap, it had to be the nicest book shop I have ever stepped inside, one of many I have been unable to resist having a browse around. Unfortunately, many of these beautiful places having to close over the years, so to find this one was a delight. Jim had found a book on Highland cattle, and I—a tiny book of poems—encased in a beautifully embroidered linen cover, dating back to 1648.

Encased between my own books, now sat Alice's herbal remedies and a plant identification guide I had brought back from my last visit; but for now, my attention returns to tonight's meal with Jim. I pull a few out, leaving Frank's 'Domestic Goddess' behind on the shelf. Watching Nigella had been one of Frank's guilty pleasures, though was never able to replicate anything she had either made on screen, or from the book I'd bought him.

Instead, preferring to succumb to her seductive charm the same way he could watch the weather forecast, hypnotised, rather than informed, completely oblivious of the impending storm! Despite being mesmerised, Frank had remarkably never fallen asleep, unlike "Bake Off", were ten minutes in, he was snoring!

Tonight, was more of a date night, rather than him returning home for a meal after a day at the office, or the field in Jim's case. If he had, as I suspect, been out and about at the farm, he will have showered, changed and spritzed before arriving. Despite retiring, as such, he still enjoyed the odd day on the farm, looking after those beasts. Maybe they even missed him as much as he did them!

The advantage of a casserole is that it can slowly take care of itself, a satisfying, yet effortless dish, allowing me time to create a dessert before immersing myself in a deep relaxing bath, along with some soothing piano music played by a very talented and dear friend of mine. Joy, had lived in the middle of nowhere, so didn't have to worry about upsetting her neighbours, although many would pay good money to hear her beautiful music. Joy, and her husband Stewart, had employed me to look after their three children, Beth, Matthew and James, all grown up with children of their own now. When I'd started, they had been in the process of restoring an old farmhouse, which in fact, was still in need of attention when I'd left, ten years later! They had provided me with a vehicle, a Land Rover series 3 SWB, perhaps the only vehicle that could survive the rough track that led to their isolated house, other than a tractor! A pair of wellies had also been an essential requirement, worn to and from the house; your presentable footwear, kept in the car for when you reached your destination. A phrase book would have also come in handy, unable to understand the odd shepherd waving me down to tell me, 'Yows ont road!' Was I not meant to be on the road! Realising, as I turned the corner, that he had perhaps been trying to warn me that his female sheep were loose on the road. I could never decide if Beth was learning to talk when she asked if we were "Gon wam", or simply picking up the local dialect! Our nearest neighbours weren't visible, just flocks of sheep, who were very friendly and would follow us, one after the other. The only other people I ever saw, was the odd rambler, following the path around the back, perhaps another reason the sheep were so pleased to see us, and why I hadn't yet bumped into Mr Right! But Joy and Stewart had loved the location and isolation, and I had fallen in love with their enthusiasm, more importantly their beautiful children, plus of course the idea of a new vehicle, unaware it had been a necessity, rather than a luxury, failing to realise the enormity of living somewhere as remote as that. I should have known the moment I set eyes on the huge pile of logs outside the front door, yet another requirement if you were to survive the cold bleak winters, in their remote seclusion. Unlike the sheep, Jim's sensitive cows would have struggled out there at the best of times. This was also relatively new to Joy and Stewart, though they'd embraced it whole heartedly, even coming home with an orphaned lamb one day, which in turn became Matthew's pride and joy, spending many hours, even days, pampering her prior to a local show, just as Beatrix Potter had. As he got older, purchasing a few more, until the day he could have his own flock. He, now like Sam, is taking over his father-in-law's farm, his wife having no brothers. Swopping the rolling dales for the more rugged fells of the Lake District National Park.

Once the children had started school, we had had a seven-mile journey to the nearby town. Despite my good intentions, I had found getting all the children ready to leave the house at the same time, to be a bit like herding sheep. On the odd occasion we did manage to leave on time, the sheep would decide to amble across the road in front of us, or a tractor delay us. Once there, we then had the arduous task of finding somewhere to park. The other parents had assumed I was the children's mother, never seeing them with her, inviting myself and my husband round for brunch with the children at the weekends. Once my status had been established, I was either welcomed with open arms as a potential babysitter, thinking I might like to look after their children in my spare time, or as well as the three in my charge! There are however, only so many children and animals you can fit in a Land Rover! Or I was simply dismissed on the basis they might lose their husbands! Other people must have also naturally assumed I was the mother, their own, rarely seen or recognised, other than with their father. At the time, causing gossip and bewilderment amongst the local community, more so when I eventually left, assuming the mistress had then taken my place!

Myself, having disappeared without a trace, leaving the children behind, despite having been so devoted to them. Perhaps I had died, out in that awful winter, whilst tending to their, or the animals every needs. By then we had five hens, a cat, a dog, four sheep, woodlice, that crept in from under the pile of logs outside, and the occasional mouse! The cat had been brought to deter the mice, but once she had obliterated these, she'd brought more home, some dead, some still alive to torment before supper! Or I could, quite simply, have gone mad, with just these to talk to!

It was a long while before I had gone back to visit, and expect people wouldn't even have recognised me without the same young children in tow. Just as someone had once believed me to be the mother of a baby I was pushing in a pram, saying how much she looked like me. I hadn't had the heart to correct her. Goodness only knows where that led!

Looking back now, all this may explain why I didn't get approached by young eligible gentlemen, as they would have naturally assumed I was a happily married woman. Not that there were many, the town was full of schoolboys from the public school there, and closer to home there had been the tramp, who, according to the children, had bedded down in a Shepard's hut, and under no circumstances, were we to give him a lift into town. Despite this handicap though, I did have the occasional date. Once the vet had realised I wasn't the children's mother, suddenly found me more attractive, until he met Matthew, with whom he seemed to have much more in common! In those days there was no internet, let alone Tinder. Had I wanted to talk on the phone, this was plugged in the hall, for all to hear, or a trek into town to the phone box, not an attractive option on a cold winter's night. Even the postman was reluctant to deliver our mail—I swear he would save up the post—waiting till we met at the end of the road, to save him negotiating the potholes! Then, the years had slipped away, without me even realising that time had run out to have children of my own.

'Perfect timing!' I declare to Jim, as he arrives.

'Something smells good,' he declares as he kisses me.

'I hope you're not saying I smell of sausages,' I retort.

'No, you smell divine, but I am hungry,' he concludes, as he follows me into the kitchen.

Who says the way to a man's heart isn't through his stomach!

Chapter 13
Sons of Our Fathers

No matter how often we strolled along the beach together with the children, whether the tide was in, or on its way out, Luke would, without fail, be wet through before we left. Whereas Lizzie, on the other hand, would tread more cautiously in her brother's footsteps, preferring to care for her baby dolls. Despite allowing all the girls I had looked after, the same opportunities as the boys, I had generally found this the case, with the exception of Daisy: Jenny and George's daughter, who had absolutely loved the outdoors, spending most of her time wearing her wellies, if she wasn't in these, then, more often than not, in a pair of football boots, handed down from her older brothers. She had loved nothing more than to chase around after the ball with the boys at the after-school club, unattended by her brothers, and would even attend the week-long football classes during the school holidays, always in the winter months in the cold and wet, gaining medals and trophies. This had all changed when she'd turned eleven, when she'd swapped her boots for heels and preferred her nails clean and polished.

Luke, I expect would love growing up in the dales, amongst all the wildlife, not forgetting all the mud! Never happier than outside, in his blue dinosaur wellies. I'm not entirely sure where I see him in the future, but he will no doubt be leading the cross-country team, maybe even surfing the waves, once he has mastered the art of swimming. Matthew had loved all things outdoors, and before caring for real livestock, had played with a toy farm yard, gathering the sheep from the shag pile rug, before transporting them back to the yard, piled one on top of the other in a trailer pulled by his John Deere tractor. His brother James, had been more content watching the world go by from inside, sat on a cushioned window seat on the half landing, sketching his thoughts and the wildlife around. He had continued to study as we all expected, and now enjoys a career in illustrating all manner of books, and the occasional Christmas card. Their sister Beth, married a public schoolboy from the nearby town, now a mother herself to baby Joshua, before which, she had baked and decorated celebration cakes. She had always enjoyed baking, even the simplest of biscuits, rolling her sleeves up and cutting out shapes, rabbits for Easter and stars for Christmas, always delicious and beautifully decorated.

Moving on from the farm, once the children had all started school and there being no sign of any more babies, I'd handed in my car keys, having accepted a new position with another young family, with a baby on the way. This time with more experience, not only in looking after young children, but in choosing a more desirable location and model of car. This appointment was in the heart of a small village, just a few miles from the nearest market town, located in the smallest county in England. It had come with another Land Rover, but this time an upgrade to a Discovery, with leather upholstery, sun roof and sound system, and the advantage of being able to drive it. Poppy had been on the verge of starting secondary school when I'd eventually left, now a successful business woman, having followed her passion for dressmaking, now altering clothes, always busy, especially in the month of May, not only altering the May Queen's dress, but responsible for making sure all the school girls fit into their glamorous gowns to attend their prom. She had also earned a reputation for altering designer bridal gowns, often working long into the night to fulfil her obligations and the wishes of these young women, which I imagine wouldn't have been a problem for Poppy, displaying nocturnal tendencies as a child. The paints and glitter had been packed away a long time ago, along with any dreams Charles may have had of becoming an artist, showing great potential as a young child, until he upset his mother by decorating the dining room walls in red glitter paint! If only she could have appreciated his long brush strokes and the occasional splashes of colour, before he'd covered it all up with black paint! Neither of us able to completely remove it without a trace, despite several coats of Dulux Jurassic Stone. Charles had always liked adding texture to his paint, experimenting with different materials: sand, biscuit crumbs, even sawdust from the bottom of Simba's cage, not that they held a lion captive! Simba, had been an adorable breed of rabbit with a lion's main. If only Charles had had his mother's blessing, he could now be displaying his works in the Tate Modern, along with "Matisse" and "Picasso", making thousands of pounds for his modern art. Despite being held responsible for the decorating debacle, this hadn't been the cause of my sudden departure. It had transpired that Tilly, their youngest daughter, hadn't been the only female in the family to have chased after Tom, their gardener!

This had led me to my final appointment, with Agatha, Faith and Hugh, all still young when I'd left with Frank, taking me into retirement and a life beyond my wildest dreams.

Jim believing farming was always in his blood, growing up with it, had never considered anything else, or regretted it. Just as Sam is continuing the tradition, working on the same farm his great grandfather had, adopting the same way of life. Not everyone would want these constraints or be lucky enough to retain their roots and traditions, making new lives and memories elsewhere. At the end of the day, home is where the heart is, and my heart belongs here. Sarah also realising this, returning here to bring up her family. If she takes after her mother, then she must have been an amazing woman, and would be very proud of her daughter.

Grace has also inherited some of her grandmother's knowledge, growing fresh herbs in her tiny garden, and loves nothing better than a glass of refreshing mint tea. I myself, like Lizzie, had as a young child, enjoyed playing and caring for my baby dolls, before Frank had opened my eyes to what lay beyond the garden gate. I had been an only child, perhaps it had been this, and the abandonment from a young age, that had instilled a longing to care for young children, just as Sophie had for me. Then as time had passed, satisfying my own need for a baby, never realising this at the time, until time had run out for me to nurse a baby of my very own. How different things would be now, if I could go back and do it all again, but that is the great mystery of life, that only becomes apparent with wisdom and age, by which time it is usually too late.

Just as we follow in the footsteps of our fathers, so does nature, the birds already beginning to return from their winter sun, the early ones, not only catching the worm, but securing the most desirable bachelor pad for a summer romance. Left sitting pretty when the rest arrive. Jim's cows, however, are still sitting pretty and being pampered under shelter, despite new born lambs skipping around the fields. Of course, this all depends on where you are in the country. Matthew's flock waiting till April to lamb outside. Previous generations having found, any sooner and they might not survive the winter weather. Just like the birds, returning to the same spot, generation after generation.

Chapter 14
Everything Stops for Tea

As promised, Sarah had taken me to Kate's cafe, it being even more divine than I'd pictured it, and very popular. An assortment of temptingly sweet treats, all beautifully decorated, displayed on the counter under glass-covered cake stands, before being served on the tiniest and most delightfully decorated assortment of fine china plates, along with both a cake knife and fork. Instead of a paper serviette, Kate had a collection of beautifully embroidered napkins, some of which she had embroidered herself.

The array of tea had also been a delight, from the humble builder's brew, to an elegant cup of Darjeeling, the fresh leaves served in their own little teapot, along with a silver strainer, adding to the sense of ceremony, whilst paying homage to these delicate leaves. Once the fashionable drink of the day, enjoyed by upper class ladies, dressed for the occasion in extravagant gowns and hats, always in a fine china cup and saucer, and never a tea bag seeped in a mug, becoming more popular and affordable in the eighteenth century. Now an integral part of our daily lives, the first cup of the day a familiar ritual, prepared as we gather our thoughts after tumbling out of bed in the morning, still bleary eyed in our pyjamas. Then perhaps a pot to share with friends, or all to oneself for those treasured moments of solitude, curled up on the sofa with a good book.

Today I was visiting on my own, to immerse myself once again in this beautiful ritual, and to deliver an old tea set acquired from Alice's house, surplus to the requirements of Sophie, Grace or myself. Despite being beautiful, none of us able to accommodate or need any more china, all now suitably equipped to host a street party! Kate pleased with my donation, especially as it was a complete set, and that I'd agreed to help bake and decorate cupcakes on a regular basis for her. Something I was more than happy to do, not normally having the opportunity to indulge my passion.

Even today, cold and wet, people had ventured out for a cup of Kate's delightful tea, having chosen from the vast array on display in glass jars, all labelled like bottles of wine, with their origin and a description. After consulting Kate, I decide to try a pot of Darjeeling Castleton Moonlight Oolong tea, mellow and fragrant, with a slight peach sweetness and lingering honey note, whose tips are picked under the light of the moon. A change from my usual Camomile! The walls, full of books, just waiting to be opened and loved again, some with messages of hope and love, now a forgotten memory. When I'd last arrived with Sarah, Kate's mother had just been leaving, having seemed pleased to bump into her, enquiring after Jim. Sarah, on the other hand, had seemed less pleased, quite cold in fact, not at all the welcome I would've expected from her.

The advantage of a pot of tea is it lasts longer than a cup, remaining warm, whilst enjoying not only the taste, but the beautiful fragrance of the leaves, along with a slice of my favourite baked cheesecake, baked by Kate, and a book from the shelf beside me—a guide to the Cornish language, still quite a mystery to me, but one I should have considered learning the moment I'd walked into the post office, never really understanding Hugh, the post master, making polite conversation. Another mystery I couldn't quite comprehend, was how a little Irish song book had found its way onto a shelf, here in Cornwall!

Chapter 15
Silver and Gold

Despite still early March, not yet officially spring, the sun had felt warm on my face whilst tidying the garden and enjoying a nettle tea from the first shoots. The daffodils now standing tall, below the first tight buds of pink blossom on the cherry tree at the bottom of the garden.

    I change before going out, deciding to choose something more colourful to match the season, finally able to abandon my woolly hat and gloves, if not yet my coat and boots. I pick up my parcel and head back out into the sunshine. I had wrapped up a novel I had just finished, the fact that it had taken a little longer to finish than usual, was no reflection on the book, just that an early night with Jim was more appealing! Instead of donating it to Kate's cafe, I had wrapped it up for Jenny, slipping a letter inside, along with my love and best wishes. It wouldn't matter to Jenny that I'd already read the book, in fact, better one that I'd enjoyed, rather than one I couldn't recommend, and like me, she enjoyed a good romance. I had spoken to George her husband last night, who'd informed me that she'd not been feeling too well. Nothing serious, but was resting, and would call me when she started to improve. I had offered my help, but George assured me he was quite capable, especially now he'd retired, taking care of Jenny's every need, promising to keep me informed and to ask if he needed my help. Jenny and I had remained good friends over all these years, ever since she'd helped mend my broken heart.

    Despite having brought the book explaining the Cornish language home with me, I had yet had little time to study it, regrettably now, as Hugh, would no doubt want to share his delights with me, hopefully nothing that required my opinion! You would think by now, I would be able to make sense of it all, but then, even Hugh had admitted he didn't consider himself Cornish! Despite having lived in the county all his life, he had actually been born in a hospital over the border! Fortunately, despite Jim being a local farmer, I could understand him, though I suppose having the advantage of understanding his body language helped! Jim, celebrating his birthday next week, is a typical Pisces, a lot like Frank, romantic and passionate, and a perfect match for a charismatic Libran like me.

Jim had lacked enthusiasm when I'd first mentioned a party to celebrate his birthday, admitting he'd already celebrated his sixtieth. But Sarah and I had won him round. Why should children have all the fun, though as a child I had only ever experienced the one. Having given into my demands, my mother had reluctantly organised, with the help of Sophie, a party for my eighth birthday, and lived to regret it, someone having got over excited whist sat on my mother's favourite chair! Needless to say, it was the first and last ever party I remember in our household. I had, nevertheless, still been invited to several others, along with Felicity, whose identity had always remained a suspicion after wetting herself at Brownie camp, but never proved. I was, however, always careful to check any seat before sitting down, which of course never allowed me to win musical chairs, but did ensure a dry party dress!

I have of course had plenty of experience over the last few decades at hosting children's birthday parties, which have always proved very popular, if not legendary, especially my treasure hunts and epic cakes, always enjoyed, and never taken home in a soggy serviette! To this day, choosing a house party over what has now become the modern-day alternative. The cost of which, I suppose nominal, compared to the insurance premium on the contents of one's home. At least then, you can come home at the end of the day, knowing you can relax in comfort!

Whilst baking for Kate, I was also able to bake for Jim's party: more cupcakes, and a large chocolate caterpillar, filled with caramel, apparently, Jim's favourite! Once I'd returned from delivering a very tempting array of cakes to Kate, I hastily began baking savoury pies and flans for this evening's festivities. Before I knew it, everything was prepared and ready to go, including myself, if a little fraught! The party was to be held at

Jim's, Sarah had thought the party a wonderful idea and had arranged a babysitter, so she and Henry could enjoy the celebrations, volunteering to address the music.

Jim helped me in with my overnight case and the food, pleased to see me, the house: as warm and inviting as Jim's embrace. We'd decided to host Jim's party at his house, as he only had the cows to upset. I've never yet encountered a neighbour who complained about children partying, it seems they're able to make as much noise as they like, whereas adults are expected to act their age!

Kate was in the kitchen, having herself, just arrived home, full of compliments for the cupcakes I'd previously left with her. Sam appears moments later, having just settled the cows after milking, heading straight upstairs for a shower, but not before greeting his wife.

'Had a good day love?' he asks, before giving her a quick kiss.

'Yes, busy though!' she replies.

'Do you mind if I jump in the shower first?' he asks.

'No, you go up. I'll see you up there,' Kate assures him.

It isn't long before Linda and Bob arrive, full of cheer, and laden with beer.

'Jim, happy birthday mate!' Bob greets, shaking his hand.

'Happy birthday! Is this going to be an annual thing?' Linda enquires, giving Jim a quick kiss on his cheek.

'Wasn't my idea,' Jim retorts.

'It's a brilliant idea! Why should little ones have all the fun?' Linda adds.

'My sentiments exactly,' I say, joining them.

There was a knock at the door, Kate, opening it on her way through, inviting in another couple, a little older than Jim and myself, neither of whom I recognise. Jim coming forward to introduce us, 'Judith, Michael, meet Molly.'

'Lovely to meet you. It's nice to be able to put a face to a name,' I say, looking into Michael's eyes for a twinkle, having only ever imagined him as 'Danny's father', as portrayed by Roald Dahl. Nothing other than his interest in pheasant shooting to go on. Judith, I could only consider to be his new wife, Danny having now grown up! Jim hadn't shared much about her, just as Judith herself gave little away, other than the outfit she'd arrived in: a pair of black trousers, sensible shoes and a drab top! I, on the other hand, loved any opportunity to dress up, slip on my heels, jangle my jewellery and lift my mood. I can still remember the excitement as a young child, changing into a pretty party dress, and the smell of my new school blazer as I joined Frank at secondary school. It was only when Michael and Judith spoke, that I realised they were a match made in Heaven, unable to understand a word either of them were saying! I stopped and considered for a moment that these people would be making their own opinion of me tonight, even my suitability, perhaps comparing me to Jim's late wife, at which, I turned to collect my glass as Sarah arrived in the kitchen with Kate, having left Henry talking to Sam and Harry in the living room.

'Are the children asleep?' I enquire.

'Eventually!' Sarah sighs. 'Luke was quite disgruntled he couldn't attend. I had to explain that tonight was for grown-ups, and that I hadn't been invited to his friend's party the other week.'

'It's my mum's birthday next week,' Kate begins. 'If I'd known earlier, they could have had a joint birthday party. But Dad had already planned to take her out.'

'What a shame,' I quip, 'though I struggled convincing Jim to agree to a party of his own, so I'm not sure how he would have felt about a joint one!' Dispelling any plans for such a future event. Whether Kate thought it a good idea or not, I certainly couldn't imagine anything worse! Kate leaving the room after refreshing her glass.

'Well saved!' Sarah sighs.

'I get the feeling, you don't exactly like Kate's mother?'

'Is it that obvious?' Sarah ventures.

'It's just that you've given me that impression occasionally,' I comment.

'Has Dad not said anything to you yet?'

'About what?' I ask, intrigued.

'Obviously not,' Sarah concludes. 'Forget it. Don't say anything to him, you'll only spoil his evening.'

'I won't,' I reassure her, wondering what could have upset her. But for now, Jim's happiness, and that of his guests is paramount, as well as satisfying their appetites. I glance over to Jim, who is smiling, leaning against the island with a glass of beer in his hand, whilst listening to Bob. Kate is relaxing in front of the fire with her new husband—in Jim's living room rather than their own. Perhaps a change, really is as good as a rest, even if it is just across the hallway! Sarah is chattering away to Linda, who is obviously amused, almost bent double, laughing. Apparently, children laugh, on average, three hundred times a day! Something Michael and Judith could do to remember, whilst engrossed in their own little world, straight faced and serious.

'I love you Miss Molly!' Jim whispers in my ear. 'You were right, it was a wonderful idea. Everyone's enjoying themselves.'

'Not sure everyone is!' I indicate towards Michael and Judith.

'They don't get out much,' Jim informs me.

'You could have fooled me!' Giving him a kiss on his cheek. 'I'm glad you're enjoying yourself. Take everyone into the other room will you, while Sarah and I put the food out, and make sure everyone's got a drink, especially those two over there.'

Sarah and I fill the island with savoury treats and a pile of plates, saving the cakes for later.

A moment later, Jim appears with yet another fellow farmer, Gabriel, from a little further afield, along with his new partner Eleanor. Jim had filled me in on these two, so well in fact, that I almost recognise Eleanor the moment I set eyes on her, immaculately dressed, with the most amazing finger nails. I should perhaps introduce her to Judith!

Gabriel's wife had apparently left when their youngest daughter had gone off to university, having preferred a brand-new house and a city bloke in a suit, to Gabriel in his overalls and wellies in a cold damp farmhouse, with the odd dead bird awaiting its fate. Gabriel, by all accounts, also liked to shoot. Eleanor on the other hand, had obviously found the combination rather attractive. He did however scrub up well, and together, they made an attractive couple.

'Hi, I hope you're hungry,' I say. 'You're just in time for some food.'

'We're ravenous!' replies Eleanor. 'This looks lovely. Thank you for inviting us both, I haven't met many of Gabriel's friends yet.'

Linda had arrived in the kitchen, obviously hungry, or on the trail of Gabriel's new-found love, introducing herself on arrival.

'Lovely to meet you. I'm Linda, the new Mrs Clifton.'

'Hi!' Eleanor replies. 'Yes, I suppose we're all starting over again. You, Molly and myself, all second time around. Sixty must be the new forty I guess!'

'How old does that make you then?' Gabriel asks her.

Obviously, Eleanor hadn't been briefed on my situation, and before I had time to correct her on my age, and my marital status, she was already enquiring about my fertility and Kate's parenthood.

'No, Kate isn't my daughter,' I manage to inform her whilst she pauses, very briefly for thought.

'So, where are yours then?' she enquires, glancing around.

'I don't have any children,' I enlighten her.

'None at all?' Eleanor replies, a little lost for words, obviously assuming every woman of a certain age has a brood of children and been married a lifetime!

'So, you were a career woman?' she continues to pry.

'I suppose I was,' I conclude, before adding how very fond of Jim's grandchildren I am.

Eleanor being quick to add, 'Oh, I've not reached that stage yet!'

I wasn't about to explain that I now had four gorgeous grandchildren. It only goes to show that things are not always what they seem, and you never know what deep secrets lie untold in the lives of the people you encounter. My mind already working overtime as to what could have upset Sarah so much for her not to like Kate's mother.

'You're spoiling him,' remarks Linda. 'You'll be giving Bob ideas, it's his birthday next month.'

'What better excuse!' I volunteer.

'Oh, I wouldn't know where to begin,' Eleanor adds, taking a chunk of cold pie. 'I must get some of this, where did you buy it Molly?' she enquires. 'It's delicious!'

'I made it. I can let you have the recipe if you like.'

'Oh, that won't be necessary, we get everything delivered,' she adds hastily.

I can see Linda raising her eyebrows, out of the corner of my eye. I imagine Eleanor's mind boggled at the thought of the process involved in making a pie. Probably never realising it possible in a domestic kitchen, though I did wonder, if it was at all possible to rub pastry with her nails!

'You know, you're very talented,' Eleanor continues.

'I bet you made everything,' Linda observes.

'Is it that obvious?' I ask, a little embarrassed.

'No, it's a compliment,' she insists. 'Far nicer than anything shop bought.'

'Thank you,' I stand corrected.

'I totally agree, you could go into business,' Eleanor suggests.

'I had never considered it a talent. You should give it a try,' I suggest. 'Just basic stuff really, though I don't normally cater on this scale.'

'You can invite us round for tea anytime,' Eleanor continues, helping herself to some rice salad. Leaving me imagining if the same pie would be quite as attractive served up with mash and peas.

I suddenly realise I haven't seen Michael or Judith for a while, so excuse myself and go in search of them.

'Hi, you two, are you alright?' I ask, wondering if they'd fallen asleep in here on their own in front of the fire. There's food in the kitchen if you're hungry, just go and help yourselves.'

'Thank you, we will,' Michael says. 'We were almost nodding off there for a moment.'

I left them to wake themselves up, a little bewildered as to how anyone could fall asleep at a party, considering how little they'd had to drink! Perhaps Sam had slipped a little something in after meeting them!

Jim had been a little embarrassed about receiving any presents, so I had suggested our guests bring something to share instead, leaving them to consider the options. Linda hadn't been able to resist bringing their wedding photos, plus a framed photo of Jim and I from their special day, a first for the mantel piece, and maybe of many. She'd also slipped me some old school photos of Jim as a child, including several that Bob must have given her of Jim in his teenage years growing up on the farm. Not having known him then, it was a nice insight into his childhood and youth. I thanked her for her thoughtfulness, suggesting a game of charades.

'Wonderful idea!' she agrees.

Even Judith joined in, illustrating the Pink Panther. Just seeing her out of character was hilarious! Until Jim guessed correctly, spoiling all our fun.

Eleanor was an amazing actress, and dancer, everybody clueless, or so it seemed, involving all the men into her routine. Judith had offered a guess, but no one, not even Michael broke the spell. She may not be able to cook, but she could certainly entertain!

It had been Sam who'd acted out "Bake Off". Being a guy, incorporating a motor bike, Kate, immediately guessing correctly. These two were obviously on the same wave length, despite being newlyweds.

Unfortunately, "Ghost" was wasted on Michael, who behaved more like a demented, innocent Casper, frolicking around.

After all that hilarity, it was time for Jim to make a wish as he blew out the candles on his birthday cake.

'I see you bought the cake then,' Eleanor whispers.

'Have you not tried it yet?' Jim asks, overhearing her comment. 'You don't get caramel filling from Marks and Spencer.

'So where did you get it?' Eleanor asks.

'I made it! I've never made a caterpillar before. Is it OK?' I ask.

'Is there no end to your talents?' Eleanor asks, between mouthfuls.

'I can't dance like you!' I admit. 'You were amazing! Where did you learn to dance like that?'

'Oh, that's just leftover baggage from my previous marriage,' she says.

Not quite sure what to say to her last comment, I ask Gabriel if they'd brought anything to the table.

'I'd considered a joint,' he says, 'but Eleanor thought it might be inappropriate, considering she hadn't met you all before.'

I honestly think he was quite serious! 'Oh, I don't know, now that I've met you all, I think it might have been fun!' Maybe, he was more attractive than I'd first imagined!

'How about we do my game?' Sarah suggests. 'We can't stay too long. We have to get back for the babysitter, unfortunately.'

How quick we grow up and accept responsibilities, it couldn't have been that long ago since she was enjoying the freedom of owning her own house, a period so short lived, before children dominated their lives. Most parties in their house now, would probably include jelly and balloons. Many couples their age, slipping quietly into middle age, becoming responsible adults, leaving the children to enjoy all the fun. Perhaps always being around children, I had a different outlook on life. Jim had certainly found it quite refreshing, and was obviously enjoying his party, despite his reservations.

Sarah had brought several wine bottles, their labels covered with a number for identification purposes. She explains the idea of the game is to identify the wine using taste alone, as each person is blindfolded. Pouring a little of the same wine into everyone's glass, she asks us to use our noses, explaining that without sight, our senses will focus on the smell, making them more intense, asking us to share our thoughts. Everyone it appears, in agreement that it's a red wine, several of us agreeing it has a dark chocolate aroma, Judith surprisingly, tasting a heavy fruit flavour.

'Possibly rotten!' Gabriel comments.

'Try to be serious,' Eleanor says.

'Seriously. Fermented,' Gabriel adds.

'That's part of the process, mate!' Michael enlightens him, obviously allowed to express his views whilst his wife can't see him.

'We're not talking silage here,' Eleanor reminds him. 'Think a fine bottle of Cabernet Sauvignon.'

Sarah, nearly dropping her glass, asks everyone to take a sip, 'Keep it in your mouth, and try sucking on it.' At which point both Gabriel and Eleanor nearly spit out the entire contents of their mouths.

'As if pulling it through a straw,' Sarah continues.

'The mind boggles!' Gabriel comments.

'Cherries,' Linda says.

'No, I'm getting beetroot,' Michael offers positively, now enjoying the experience.

'Don't be ridiculous, Michael!' his wife orders.

'I've finished, can I have some more?' Henry asks.

Harry, quiet up until now, declares, 'I think I prefer my beer!'

'Right, I going to take your glasses off you,' Sarah says.

'I'm sorry,' Michael says.

'No, on second thoughts,' Sarah says, 'take off your blindfolds.'

'I really am sorry,' Michael continues, apologetically.

'What's the matter Michael?' Sarah asks him.

'I didn't mean to spoil everyone's fun,' he tells her.

'What are you talking about?' Sarah asks him, with a puzzled look on her face.

'Well everyone was enjoying themselves, until I made a comment, and now we've had to stop,' he says mournfully.

'Don't be ridiculous!' Sarah tells him.

'That's exactly what Judith says,' he replies.

'No, I want you to see what you've been tasting, but with your eyes open. It'll taste differently now you can see it,' Sarah explains.

'Oh!' he smiles.

'Here,' Sarah instructs him, 'hand these around for me,' she says, handing him a plate of sliced, crusty white bread and celery.

'Where's the cheese?' Henry asks.

'There is no cheese! A little bread or celery will cleanse your palate before trying the next wine,' she advises, as Gabriel and Harry wash their bread down with their remaining wine!

'I'm watching you,' I hear Judith whisper to Michael.

'She asked me to. What was I supposed to say?'

'Right, everyone refreshed and ready to try again?'

'Were we right love?' Gabriel asks.

'Ah, sorry, I forgot,' Sarah admits.

'I thought it was us you were hoping to confuse!' Gabriel shouts.

'Right, the wine you all just tasted, was a young Cabernet Sauvignon, from South Africa,' she enlightens us.

'Oh, I would have guessed it was Tesco's finest!' Gabriel announces.

'I said that!' Eleanor shouts.

'No love, I was joking!' Gabriel tells her.

'No Gabriel, I got it right! I said it was a Cabernet Sauvignon,' Eleanor explains, making sure he understood.

'Smarty pants!' says Gabriel, smacking her bottom.

'Right if you all put your blindfolds back on, we can proceed to the next wine. Everybody ready?'

'Is it this much fun in the bedroom?' Gabriel enquires. Obviously, the wine now having an effect, on his already loose tongue.

'If you're good, I'll let you take your masks home with you tonight,' Sarah says, much to everyone's amusement. Everyone that is, except Judith. Even Michael, I notice, displaying a little smirk, before catching his wife's eye! Jim catching my eye, giving me a wink.

'Right, tell me what you think?' Sarah asks, once we've all composed ourselves.

'I think we should go home after this!' Henry starts.

'Oh, early night for someone!' Gabriel shouts.

'It's cold,' Linda comments.

'Good, what could that tell us?' Sarah asks.

'You've just got it out of the fridge,' Gabriel offers.

'Possibly a white,' Bob adds.

'We've just got a new silver one, cracking, isn't it love?' Gabriel says, back in full flow, opening his mouth before engaging his brain!

'Yes, it can fit a complete shop in it!' Eleanor continues, obviously losing the plot!

'Not the complete shop,' Gabriel continues to inform us.

'No, I didn't mean it like that,' she continues, now in a little world of their own. 'Just what the delivery men bring.'

'What, even your amazon deliveries?' Linda now asks.

'No, just perishables,' Eleanor says.

Laughter now resounding the room, Sarah asks us to consider the wine for a moment.

'Light,' I offer.

'Good, thank you Molly,' Sarah says, relieved we're now back on track.

'Floral,' Judith adds quietly.

'Fruity,' Eleanor suggests.

Gabriel unable to resist nipping her bottom, judging by her little squeal of delight, obviously nipping the right bottom!

'Full bodied,' Gabriel offers, obviously veering off track again!

'Fragrant,' I suggest, not altogether sure if it's the wine, or Eleanor's perfume I can smell!

'Try sipping it again,' Sarah advises us.

'Gooseberries,' I hear Henry say.

'Good Henry. I think you're getting it.'

'Oh, favouritism now!' says Gabriel. 'Teacher's pet!'

'Any more suggestions?' Sarah asks, before describing the region of New Zealand the grapes are grown in to produce this Sauvignon Blanc, before accepting defeat, deciding that Henry was probably right, and they should be going home.

'I was going to try a dessert wine, with music,' Sarah informs me. 'Did you know, high frequency sounds can affect the sweetness?'

'I think this is about all they can absorb this evening,' I conclude, before she bids us all farewell, thanking me for a lovely evening, and wishing her father a happy birthday, before heading home with Henry.

The party continuing long into the early hours of the following morning, and us eventually having to wake Michael and Judith up from their slumber on Jim's sofa, all the excitement perhaps having been too much for them. We had considered leaving them both there, but Linda had arranged for a couple of taxis to deliver everyone home safely, leaving just Jim and I to lock the door behind us, and climb the stairs, wearily, but happily, to bed. The masks would have to keep for another night!

Chapter 16
Never Judge a Book by Its Cover

'Good morning,' I mutter, rolling over towards Jim.
'Is it morning already?' Jim asks, stirring from his slumber.
'It was morning when we got to bed, if you remember,' I remind him.
When we had eventually got up, and washed all the glasses, without breaking any, we went for a stroll on the beach to blow away the cobwebs.
'I think last night was a success. Don't you?' Jim asks.
'Just as long as you enjoyed yourself. It was your party,' I say.
'I did. Why, don't you think anyone else did?' he questions.
'Everyone, apart from your mate Michael, and his miserable wife,' I inform him.
'I hadn't really noticed,' Jim says.
Judith could have had eyes for Jim, and he'd never notice! Perhaps that had been the case, and I'd spoilt her fun!
'You should never judge a book by its cover,' Jim eventually says.
'I disagree,' I add. 'Surely first impressions are a good indication. Isn't it what attracts you to a person in the first place?' I argue.
'Perhaps she had other things on her mind,' Jim offers, excusing her behaviour.
'Like what?' I ask, unable to comprehend.
'Judith accused Michael of flirting with Kate's mother at a recent charity ball,' he enlightens me. 'Of course, he hadn't been.'
'You would say that!' I say, in Judith's defence, recalling her behaviour the previous evening.
'You have met Kate's mother!' Jim reminds me.

'Now you come to mention it,' I say.

'But wouldn't you then expect Judith to up her game, make more of an effort, to stop his eyes wandering. Or has she always been like that?' I ask.

'She is who she is, I suppose. Take it or leave it.'

'Well, if that's as good as it gets, I'm not surprised his eyes wandered. She's just a bit dull in my opinion,' I conclude.

'Well, that certainly can't be said about you,' he says, putting his arm around me. 'You're full of surprises!'

'Variety is said to be the spice of life,' I quote.

'You certainly bring that to the table,' he adds.

'Don't forget my pie, and chocolate cake!'

'Is that why Sarah doesn't seem to like Kate's mother?' I ask.

'I don't understand?' Jim says.

'Because she upset Judith?' I ask.

'Something like that,' Jim says dismissively.

'Well, at least I know now if I bump into her in Tesco,' I conclude. One thing's for sure, I won't be bumping into Eleanor there anytime soon! Fortunately for their sake we're not all alike, relying on them to provide us with every ingredient to sustain us, even ready-made meals in Eleanor's case, delivered to their door. Perhaps never considering the origin of what she buys, or the ethicalities, whilst farmers in this country are giving over a proportion of land around their fields, providing hedge way highways to encourage wildlife and their habitats, not only protecting the countryside, but also the future of the world's food supply.

'Is Sarah all right?' I ask Jim.

'As far as I know,' he says. 'Why do you ask?' he continues, a little concerned.

'Just that I never saw her drink last night. Even when she was doing the wine tasting.'

'No, you wouldn't. She never drinks and drives, never did. Just now, she doesn't even trust taxi drivers, or anyone else behind a wheel for that matter.'

'I'd never considered that,' I admit. There was I thinking she might be pregnant, when I couldn't have been further from the truth.

'Shall we go back and grab some lunch?' I suggest. 'There's even some cake left for afters.'

'Sounds perfect,' Jim agrees, taking my hand.

The following day was Mother's Day, mothers, young and old across the country celebrating with their children. Jim and I were in his kitchen, preparing lunch for Sarah, Henry and the children, who were enjoying a Sunday off, joining us after the church service. Sam and Kate having lunch with her parents. Jim opened the wine, a bottle of Pinot Grigio someone had brought the other night, as I set the table.

'We're here!' Sarah shouts, arriving through the door. 'I'm feeling completely spoilt today,' she admits. 'Thank you for this Molly.'

'Not at all, it's my pleasure,' I tell her. 'You deserve it.'

The meal was perfectly cooked and gratefully received. Sarah, even enjoying a glass of wine. Henry a glass of water.

'Grandma,' Luke begins, 'do you live here now?'

'I don't live here Luke. But I sometimes stay,' I inform him.

'Like a sleepover?' Luke questions.

'Yes, if it's too late to go home,' I explain.

'Where do you sleep?' he continues.

'Upstairs.'

'No, I mean in which bed?' he demands.

'Next to me Luke,' Jim adds.

'That's told us!' Henry concludes.

'So, are you going to get married?' Luke continues.

At which point, I didn't quite know where to look, and without thinking, blurt out, 'Not yet Luke!'

'Sorry, Molly,' Sarah interrupts, trying to excuse her son.

'Luke, it's rather rude to ask questions like that,' she explains to him.

'But you…' Luke begins.

'Luke, no more,' she warns him.

'Do you think you might get married one day Luke?' I ask, trying to defuse the tension.

'Not if I have to share my bed!' he decides.

'I like mummy's bed,' Lizzie informs us, as if understanding everything that's been said.

'Yes, we know you do darling,' Henry adds.

'Dessert, anyone?' I ask.

'Yes please!' shouts Luke.

'Yes please!' shouts Lizzie.

'Thank the Lord!' I whisper to myself, as I carry the plates into the kitchen, enjoying a moment's solitude to collect my thoughts, and answers for round two!

'I'm so sorry Molly, I never know what he's going to come out with next, these days!' Sarah explains, following me into the kitchen.

'Don't worry,' I reassure her. 'He's only curious, and remember, I'm used to it.'

'Thank goodness!' she sighs.

'I'll have a little word with him when we get home. I seem to be doing a lot of that just recently,' she explains.

Jim had remained at the table, perhaps as perplexed as I was. Dessert was gratefully received, boosting mine, and Jim's depleted energy levels, both of us still recovering from Friday night. We might like to behave like children, but aren't quite as resilient!

Jim and I took Luke and Lizzie outside for some fresh air and to check on their calves: Star and Crocus, and the rest of the herd, now enjoying the sunshine and lush green grass; Jim having eventually allowed them out, if only during the day! Not only is the grass growing, but the trees and hedges are all in bud, having lain dormant, surviving the elements of winter. Even Jim's apple trees, invaded by mistletoe, are bursting with buds, reminding me yet again of Frank, how, despite our love having survived all those years to blossom again, his body couldn't recover from his awful cancer that had eaten away at him. His love for life, for us, even the sunshine, couldn't save him in the end, reluctantly leaving me, to watch the leaves fall, along with my tears.

'Look, Grandad,' Lizzie calls over to Jim, 'Kate's here.'

We immediately glance back towards the house to see both Kate and Sam emerging from their vehicle, acknowledging us with a wave. Luke already on their trail, with Lizzie in hot pursuit. Kate and Sam wander in our direction, Sam greeting Luke, throwing him in the air before sitting him on his shoulders. Lizzie having to trundle behind holding Kate's hand.

'Hi!' I greet them. 'Have you had a nice day?'

'Lovely, thanks,' Kate says. 'You?'

'Yes, we've left Sarah and Henry relaxing inside,' I add.

'Look Lizzie!' Kate says, bending to pick a daisy, 'let me show you how to make a daisy chain,' she explains, sitting down beside her, her own nimble fingers better equipped to the task than Lizzie's chubby little fingers and nibbled nails. Kate, as determined as ever to share and encourage Lizzie in all the things she once enjoyed as a little girl, producing a chain to crown Lizzie's head.

'Shall we go and show Mummy?' Kate asks Lizzie, enticing her inside.

'We'll follow in a minute,' Sam shouts after her.

'Look how Star's grown,' Sam tells Luke, noticeably proud.

'She's bigger than Crocus,' Luke informs us.

'It's perhaps all those nettles she's been feasting on,' Sam suggests.

'You can't eat nettles!' Luke laughs.

'You can if you're a cow,' Sam explains. 'Perhaps they tickle her taste buds!'

Luke laughs, not quite sure what to believe. Amongst the random nettles and daisies are dandelions, a favourite of mine, not only in salads, but the bright flower heads, if left, produce the most magical seed heads. Frank had liked neither, proclaiming them weeds, yet growing on his grave, is the largest dandelion I have ever seen, with the most vibrant head!

Back inside, Lizzie already settled in her mother's embrace, with her thumb in her mouth and her crown still balancing on her head, I suggest a cup of tea.

'Before you do that,' Sam says, catching Kate's eye, 'Kate and I have some news to tell you all.'

'You're not getting divorced already!' Henry exclaims.

'We're having a baby!' Sam announces.

'Well, I think that deserves more than tea, Don't you Jim?' I suggest. 'Congratulations!'

'Yes, indeed!' Jim agrees.

Henry extends his hand to Sam, as men do, in these situations, and Sarah stands with Lizzie in one arm to embrace Kate with the other.

'Your baby can have Tulip's calf when it's born,' Luke suggests to Sam.

'I think Tulip's calf will arrive before our baby,' he explains.

'So, when is it due?' Sarah asks what everyone else is thinking.

'September the twelfth,' Kate says proudly.

'Have you told your parents?' Sarah asks.

'Yes, just today,' Kate informs us. 'Mum's overjoyed!'

Jim arrives back with a tray of flutes, two filled with sparkling water, one for Kate, the other for Henry, it being Mother's Day and Sarah already having had a drink, the others bubbling with Champagne, left over from the other night.

'Congratulations!' Jim announces, raising his glass, as we all follow.

'So, this time next year, you'll be a mother yourself,' I begin, chatting to Kate, noticing Sarah leave the room with Lizzie asleep in her arms.

'Well, even Christmas,' Kate replies, excitedly.

'I'll have to get knitting,' I say, sharing in her excitement.

'Molly, I mean Grandma, will you help me?' Luke asks, sat on the floor building Lego bricks.

'What is it you're making?' I ask, sitting on the floor beside him.

'I'm making a milking parlour,' he explains. 'What can I use for the milk tanks?' he asks.

I wonder, rummaging through the pile of bricks, considering I would be more at home in an ice cream parlour than a milking parlour.

'Molly,' Henry asks, leaning forward, 'have you seen Sarah?'

'I think she went to put Lizzie down for a sleep. Do you want me to check on them? I'm nipping up to the bathroom,' I ask.

'Would you? It's just I thought we might leave soon.'

'Just as long as you help your son. Be warned though, it'll require a lot of imagination!'

Upstairs, I wander across the landing to Sarah's old bedroom where I can hear something. I creep in, expecting to find Lizzie whimpering in her sleep, but Lizzie is sound asleep on the bed and Sarah is in tears on the window seat.

'Oh Sarah, come here,' I say, sitting down beside her and gathering her into my arms, realising she must be missing her own mother.

'It's so unfair Molly,' Sarah cries. 'If it wasn't for her, Mum may still be alive.'

'I don't understand?' I say, puzzled. 'If it wasn't for who? I thought it was an accident.'

'Mum and Dad had been arguing the morning she died. Mum was upset because she'd caught Kate's mum flirting with Dad. Now she's not here to see her grandchildren, but Kate's still got her mother to share her child with, see her grandchild grow up, celebrate Mother's Day each year.'

'Does anyone else know how you feel?' I ask.

'Just Henry,' Sarah replies. 'Please don't tell Sam, or Kate.'

'I won't,' I promise.

'I get the impression Kate's mother will flirt with anyone. Surely your mother realised that. I take it your dad was innocent in all this?' I ask.

'Yes, of course,' Sarah replies.

'Then you have to try and accept what happened was an accident. Don't let it spoil the happy memories you have, or your future happiness, life's too short, trust me. Enjoy Sam's happiness, he's going to need your support, more than ever,' I try explaining, before Luke comes running in.

'Why are you crying Mummy? Are they happy tears?' he asks.

'Yes darling, they're happy tears,' she sobs, as she holds her son close. 'I love you Luke.'

'I love you too Mummy. Are you coming down now? I want to show you what Daddy and I have built.'

'I'll be there in a minute,' she assures him, wiping away her tears.

'Let's go down Luke,' I say, taking his hand. 'Show me what you've made. Mummy will be down in a moment.'

'What a day!' I sigh, once Jim and I are alone.

'I think my daughter has been getting carried away. Do you want me to have a word with her?' Jim asks.

'What?' I ask.

'About Luke's remarks earlier,' Jim reminds me.

'Oh, no, not on my account. I think she'll have realised that for herself. Can we just forget about it please?' I say, having other things on my mind.

'As long as I can share your bed tonight!' Jim continues.

'I thought I'd be staying here,' I consider, a little confused.

'What's the matter Molly, what's on your mind?' Jim asks, a little worried now.

'I don't want to interfere Jim, but Sarah was upset today. I think she's just missing her mum, she told me about the argument you had with your wife, the day she died,' I explain.

'It wasn't serious. It was just that blessed woman: Kate's mother,' Jim explains.

'I know, Sarah said. But talk to her,' I suggest.

'Is she all right?' Jim asks, concerned.

'Yes, I think so, but spend some time together. She needs you right now,' I tell him.

'Thanks Molly,' he says, kissing me.

'I wish you'd been able to have children of your own.'

'Don't say that,' I say. 'It's impossible now.'

'I know, but you would have been a wonderful mother,' he continues.

'I had the next best thing,' I conclude.

'You're the best thing that ever happened to me, Miss Molly!'

Chapter 17
Our Song

I hadn't slept well, processing all that had happened, whilst listening to the rain, reminding me of the river, and how fast time flows. Sad, Frank and I hadn't had the opportunity to conceive a child, having to remind myself of all the other wonderful times we had shared together, as children ourselves, something Kate and Sam had never had. How blessed I was to have held Frank in my arms to say goodbye. I had eventually fallen asleep, only to be disturbed by the dawn chorus, becoming more noticeable every morning, though I must be getting more used to them now, like the breeze, lulling me back to sleep.

I woke to the sunshine creeping in through the crack in the curtains, and a little hand-written note on top of my phone from Jim, asking me to call him once I was awake.

'Hi Jim,' I say, when he answers his phone, 'I didn't hear you wake.'

'I'm glad. I didn't want to disturb you, you looked so peaceful,' he informs me.

'I didn't sleep well,' I tell him. 'I hope I didn't disturb you.'

'No, but you should have done. Stay where you are, I'm on my way,' he instructs me.

I did in fact quickly visit the bathroom to freshen up, before jumping back in bed to get warm before Jim joined me, where we continued to remain for the rest of the morning.

Friday morning arrived, and as planned I was now on my way to celebrate Lucy's fifth birthday before leaving on Monday to cruise along the Danube with Jim. Lucy was already enjoying her party tea under the shelter of the chestnut tree at the bottom of the garden when I arrived, just in time for her to make a wish as she blew the candles out on her cake and sing happy birthday. Lucy enjoying being the centre of attention, as always, allowed me to spend a bit of time with William before her friends went home.

The children, having retired earlier than usual, meant Grace and I had the evening to ourselves; Jack, her husband being away on business.

'Look what Sophie found,' Grace begins, opening a box. 'They belonged to my dad. Grandma must have kept them all these years. I wonder if my dad knew!'

'They were obviously special to your grandma, not necessarily to your dad,' I explain. 'I'm not quite sure he would remember that!' I say, as Grace produces a blue plastic rattle in the shape of a rocking horse.

'Now, there's something I do remember,' I smile, as Grace hands me an old white T shirt. 'It even smells of him!' I say, holding it to my face, remembering Frank wearing it, taking me back to those summer days we'd cycle to the tennis courts together. 'You mustn't throw this away,' I instruct her.

'You can have it Molly. It obviously means something to you,' she says. 'The thing is they're not my memories. I realise they were part of his life, but one I didn't know, wasn't even part of. I have different memories: his leather-soled shoes walking on the wooden floor in the hallway, alerting me he was home. The smell of his after shave when I gave him a hug, and the mug he drank his tea from in the morning before leaving for work.'

'I hope you kept it,' I say. 'To remind you.'

'No, I didn't,' Grace tells me. 'I don't need them, I'll never forget some things, or at least I hope I won't.'

'Now why would he have kept this?' Grace asks, revealing a tattered old Shakespeare volume.

'He kept it!' I exclaim, realising I probably still had mine somewhere. 'He would probably still be able to recite 'act 5, scene 1', if you were able to ask him,' I inform her, remembering how we'd learnt each and every act, whilst sat on the river in our little boat, just like the words to a song, gaining us each a grade one in literature. It was just a pity, neither of us grasped the fundamentals of the French language!

'Who's this?' Grace asks.

I take the photo from her, and for a moment remain speechless. He'd kept a picture of me, slipped between the pages, a school photo from fourth year. 'It's me!' I reply.

'Of course! I can see that now,' Grace smiles. 'How sweet! I think we both need a drink,' Grace says, getting up and wandering into the kitchen, leaving me alone with my thoughts and memories, realising that everyone's memories are individual and special to that time in their life, etched in our hearts to cherish. I begin wondering what might have happened to our little boat, hoping someone else had had pleasure from it, just like the couple making new memories in Frank's old house. Unlike the old properties in a nearby coastal resort, being knocked down or changed beyond all recognition, not only destroying the character of the village, but the very soul. Once a family home, full of memories, children waking up on Christmas morning, running around barefoot in the garden, the smell of homemade scones. What might the families feel if they were to return and find their veranda gone, where they'd once sat in their rocking chair watching the sun go down. Worse still, the schools and churches now converted into dwellings, nightclubs or restaurants. All those souls disturbed. People cooking where couples once stood making their wedding vows, sleeping where the choir had once sung, or the bells rang out. Perhaps they can still be heard, ringing in disdain, once a sanctuary, now filled with the sound of drums being played by an adolescent occupant disturbing their peace. School walls, once full of colour, now family portraits. The playing field, once full of laughter and children running and skipping, now a building site for future generations, now having to travel further afield to the nearest school.

'Here Molly,' Grace says, handing me a glass of red wine.

'Thanks Grace,' I say, accepting the glass.

'I hadn't realised,' Grace begins, 'but I'm actually doing exactly the same thing. I've even kept Lucy's first haircut, and all their christening and birthday cards. I suppose neither of them will be interested in either when they grow up. Is this my dad?' she asks, opening a photo album.

'Yes, and me,' I realise. Sophie had obviously taken pictures of Frank and I together as children. 'Would you mind if I copied some of these?' I ask.

'You take them,' Grace insists. 'We can show them to Lucy and William when they're older.'

'Thank you, I'll treasure them,' I tell her.

I bid farewell after lunch the following day, before Grace's mother was due to arrive. I had never met her and have no desire, or need to, just as I expect she feels the same about me. Despite having loved Frank, she had fallen out of love, were as mine had remained strong. Before leaving, I first visit Alice's resting place, unfortunately carrying only a bunch of very nice supermarket flowers, my own garden being a little depleted of colour just yet. Come summer, I will be able to return with handpicked roses and dahlias from my garden. The graveyard though, is ablaze with colour, as well as clusters of daffodils and bluebells, many of the graves are displaying fresh flowers left by loved ones for their mothers, suddenly remembering I'd have to visit our church on my return. I had been asked to help with the church flowers, but unable to arrange more than a few flowers in a graveside vase, I had opted to help clean the church, more especially, the persistent bat droppings in the pews. They may be a protected species, but are clearly not facing extinction any time soon, at least not as far as our congregation are concerned!

I walked the short distance to Sophie's house, promising to call before I left. I couldn't come all this way and not see her, and as it was such a beautiful morning, I took a stroll along the river and through the woods. The bluebells were already beginning to carpet the forest floor between the trees, and the ramsons were almost fit to burst. Without thinking I found myself outside Frank's gate, the garden just as I'd remembered, the apple blossom just appearing, and the rampant rose having escaped into next doors garden. I lingered, perhaps a little longer than I should have, as out of Frank's half open bedroom window, our song was playing.

Sophie held me in her arms whilst I'd cried, just as she had when I was a child. She understood me, without me having to say anything. We enjoyed cheese on toast, just as she always made it, bubbling on top and burnt at the edges, followed by freshly baked warm scones and a cup of tea, whilst she shared the stories behind the photographs in the album. All too soon it was time for me to leave, to return to Jim and all that awaited on our adventure together.

Chapter 18
Auld Lang Syne

After an early departure, we arrived on board the boat, docked in Nuremberg, with just enough time to unpack and change for dinner, before being introduced to the captain and briefed on the events of the following day, and of course, more importantly, what to do in the event of the boat going down. Quite simply, we were to make our way to the sun deck, which would still be above water, the river never that deep!

Next began the task of remembering everyone's name. We'd already met George and his wife, neither of us able to remember her name, referring to her as Mildred, between ourselves, of course! Then Peter and Jane, more easily remembered, associating them with the reading scheme, introduced to me as a child. A beautiful couple we'd shared a table with whilst enjoying dinner, and as much wine as we liked, or what the waiter chose to pour behind our back, whilst we were engaged in conversation! Peter, informing us they'd been married ninety-four years! Of which, only three to each other, after having met at a funeral. Dessert was chosen from the trolley, delivered to us by the chef, and served with a large tipple of limoncello.

Before we knew it, it was well past our bedtime. We said our goodnights and toddled of to our bed, Jim unsure as to whether the boat was moving or not, despite the scenery remaining the same!

The following morning, we sat down to breakfast, introducing ourselves to more new faces, before visiting the impressive city, its castle and walls still intact. We crossed the suspension bridge over the river to browse the market, selling an array of goods, from baby dolls to a wide selection of dentistry tools! We of course sampled their famous gingerbread, with a coffee, whilst watching the world go by. We had also wandered along the high street, where I took the opportunity to purchase some loose clothing, and yet another bra, having been informed there had been a yoga class on the boat before breakfast, and as usual, omitting to pack a suitable one for every eventuality. The time arrived for us to leave it all behind and re-join the boat in time for her to set sail to our next destination, Regensburg.

The evening followed much the same format as the previous one, an enjoyable meal, wine and the company of another couple, this time an Australian couple, Richard, and as neither Jim or I caught his wife's name, she'll remain Judy!

I eventually fell asleep listening to Jim read to me the following days itinerary, having been informed by the cruise director that tomorrows exercise class would be using the gym equipment, starting at six-thirty am! My new bra completely unsuitable for such an activity! Despite never seeming to pack the correct underwear—I say underwear, when in fact, it is almost always possible to omit knickers, I happen to have a whole drawer at home designated to bras: strapless, nude, black, alluring, even sports, just like Frank had a drawer for his entire sock collection.

On the third day, we rose again, still sailing towards our next destination. After another hearty breakfast, and more introductions, we were entertained by the chef, demonstrating how to make a veal escalope. Then the hairdresser, who advised us, that despite his poor language skills, he was still able to give a good blow job!

After lunch and a glass of the local white wine, we disembarked to visit Weltenburg Abbey: from the outside, uninviting and rather dull, but once inside, more than spectacular! An early, lavish masterpiece, in the late baroque style, created by the Asam brothers, each depicting each other inconspicuously, in recognition of their work, like an artist's signature, or the discreet inscription on an ordinance survey map.

My eyes being first drawn to the magnificent, illuminated ceiling painting, flooded with light, leading a procession of the faithfully departed to Heaven, whilst creating the impression of a cupola. The front of the church opening towards the theatrical high alter, where the mounted figure of Saint George is rescuing the princess of Libya from being devoured by a dragon. On his right, stands Saint Martin, accompanied by his attribute, a goose.

The organ, built in 1729, we are told is the only one of its kind still working today.

Whilst visitors occupied the central pews, one couple sat to one side, beside the rich, velvet, purple drapes of the confessionals, as though awaiting their penance! We were informed of several angels depicted throughout the church, the four continents represented by the arch angels: Uriel, Gabriel, Raphael and Michael. John, the saint of bridges was identified by a halo with seven stars, depicting the seven stars that had hovered over the place where he'd drowned.

There were in fact so many capricious details to absorb in one brief visit, I was left wondering about so many elements, realising it wouldn't have mattered that the service was first held in Latin. As a child attending church, I had been more interested in the carvings at the end of the pew, imagining them to be waves.

Outside, we sat under the already blossoming Chestnut trees, originally planted to shade the cellars beneath against the sun's rays. Once the trees had become established, the beer garden had evolved for the public to sit and enjoy their beer, fresh from the barrels below. For some fellow travellers, the attraction had been alcoholic rather than spiritual, rewarded for their patience with a glass of dark, almost black beer, known as Kloster Barock Dunkel, accompanied by a very large pretzel each.

Once refreshed, we were ready to embark a smaller boat, taking us back along the Danube gorge. Then back aboard our luxury vessel in time to change for dinner, after which we were entertained by a very enthusiastic group of Bavarian dancers, accompanied by several accordion players and other musicians with a selection of hand bells. They left exhausted, in time for us to set sail as we retired to bed, not at all tired myself, having drunk what I had assumed to be decaffeinated coffee!

Day four, and an introduction to another guide, Elsa, and a musical extravaganza. Our first stop Chateau Hellbrunn, to fill our lungs with fresh air, before singing outside the summer house, just as Liesl and Rolf had done in the Sound of Music. Elsa, dressed in her Dirndl dress, informed us she had a wardrobe full of similar outfits, all different sizes, probably due to the calories she'd lost laughing! As well as being amusing, she was also very knowledgeable, talking and laughing the whole time we were travelling, informing us that Mozart, despite being considered unattractive, had had six children, and his wife, having been so in love with him, had climbed into his death bed, cradling their baby, unable to imagine life without him. His name still remembered, seen above a café, hotel and bar. Apparently after being dead a hundred years, your name can be used for whatever, assuming anyone can remember it! Elsa pointed out a hotel, in a different name, costing eight thousand pounds a night, for which, the butler will iron your newspaper, so ink won't get on your hands—I assume—after he'd pressed your white shirt!

We had of course, to retrace the steps of Maria and the Baron von Trapps seven children—under the rose arch, then around the fountain in the Mirabel Gardens, surrounded by four marble statues, symbolising the four elements, leaving under the outstretched arms of two large statues, sculpted in the late seventeenth century, today looking a little worse for wear, one in desperate need of a hip replacement! Elsa also pointed out a pressed edelweiss flower encased between glass, hanging from her neck, Switzerland's national flower, found growing in high altitudes, flourishing in calcareous gorges, were few can only get too. Edelweiss translates as noble and white, signifying love and devotion, men having fallen to their deaths in pursuit of this wild blossom! One of the group: a Japanese man, perhaps realising how rare these blossoms were, made sure he captured it for posterity. Elsa unperturbed, continued to address us, despite him invading her space! We were privileged to eat lunch in a magnificent dining room, located in the oldest restaurant in Europe, very grand, somewhere I imagine used for formal banquets, perfect even for wedding celebrations. Ourselves underdressed and out of place, hiding our backpacks under the long white linen cloths.

We set sail the following day, after visiting Melk Abbey, full of history, with the most beautiful library, somewhere I could have stayed all day. Somewhere Saint Benedict had lost all sense of time himself, having to be reminded it was Easter, a little like us on the boat, where all the days drift by, having only the cruise director to remind us each evening of the next day's activities. We followed the yellow brick road into the village, then along the river, back to the boat. Jim and I collected bikes and cycled the twenty miles or so, catching up with the boat down river, then walked into the village for a well-deserved glass of beer, before arriving back on board to prepare for more entertainment.

We disembarked the coach, unfortunately not horse drawn, in front of a magnificent palace, arriving into a very ornate entrance hall, oozing with opulent grandeur, greeted with a glass of Austrian Sekt, before enjoying an evening of Strauss and Mozart, performed by a traditional Viennese orchestra in an exquisitely decorated concert room.

Another day, another excursion, today a visit to a cultural heritage site in Vienna, home to some very beautiful horses. The highlight: to witness these very talented creatures perform marches, waltzes and graceful symphonies, in perfect harmony with the music, and with the grace and control associated with that of a ballet dancer, in the most beautiful riding arena I have ever seen.

Jim and I remained in Vienna to experience their famous coffee and delicious Sachertorte, in a traditional café, the toilets of which were hidden behind a red velvet curtain!

Our final day, and we'd arrived in Budapest, a beautiful place, full of more beautiful buildings with an exquisite array of coloured roof tiles. Jim and I wandered back along the paths, showered with pink blossom, Jim picking one and placing it in my hair. We passed two young children sat on a bench playing their violins, their cases open in front of them, probably realising this to be more productive than practising alone in their bedrooms, attracting a small crowd below. Our final stop of the day, was to listen to a piano recital in an old school, reminding me of my old school chapel, and for some reason, my French teacher Brother Dominic.

We enjoyed our final dinner, sharing a table and several bottles of Champagne and wine, with three other couples we'd met on board and become good friends with. After dinner, we put on our coats and made our way up to the sun deck as the captain sailed through the city, quite spectacular when lit up at night. Downstairs in the lounge we were entertained by a group of Hungarian dancers, and finally the on-board pianist. After a glass each of Dom Benedictine, we all decided to let our hair down and dance the night away, one last time.

Fortunately, Jim and I had packed before dinner the previous evening, leaving out our clothes to travel home in, allowing us time to enjoy breakfast one last time with our new friends. It felt nice to be making new friends with Jim, rather than inheriting each other's old friends. You can never, it seems, have too many. Unfortunately, our cases had left, after noticing I'd selected the wrong bra for the dress I was wearing, the straps exposed for everyone to see. Perhaps no one would notice after all that alcohol last night, or simply assume, I'd finally run out of clean underwear! We said a polite goodbye to Richard and Judy, before embracing our new forever friends, promising to keep in touch with each other.

Chapter 19
Edelweiss

We had finally arrived home at the end of our cruise, a lot wiser and heavier than when we'd left, now in need of a more relaxed pace of life and some more familiar faces, just in time to meet the latest addition to Jim's herd.

'What shall we call her?' Sam asks Jim.

'Can I choose a name for this one?' I ask.

'I don't see why not,' Jim says, regarding me, a little bemused. 'Let's hear your suggestion.'

'Edelweiss,' I suggest. The calf, more white than black, reminding me of the flower.

'After all, Lizzie called hers Crocus, and her mother is called Tulip, and we'll always remember her birthday!' I conclude.

The following morning, we were up bright and early again, Jim having insisted in attending a routine hospital appointment with me to obtain the results from a recent MRI scan I'd had to determine any changes to a pituitary adenoma detected last year, whilst investigating another problem. Therefore, no one knowing exactly how long it had actually been there for, or whether it would grow and need removing. The fact I was in good health led me to believe all was well, and I had continued normally.

We're directed to the waiting room, advised my consultant is running about half an hour late, although the waiting room tells a different story. We sit together quietly, not wanting to disturb the silence, so often associated with waiting rooms, 'Thin Lizzy' playing rather quietly on the radio in the background. The waiting room itself: just four chairs, side by side, on either wall, between two rooms. The couple facing Jim and I, are perhaps a little older than us, both reading newspapers; the gentleman, struggling with a broad sheet, whilst his wife—I say his wife, when in fact they could be lovers—despite her left finger adorning several bands, is engaged in the crossword in her tabloid, folded neatly across her knee. The couple beside us, on first glance, appear to be father and daughter. The appointment letter had stated a friend or family member were welcome to attend the appointment with the patient, reminding me of the day I was sat with Frank, when we had received his devastating news. What it had failed to mention was the lack of seats in the very small waiting area or reading material on offer. What there was, dated back to prince George's early days and Cheryl Coles marriage to Jean Bernard in 2014, or several free copies of the National Trust newsletter, which without anything else, I read from cover to cover, even an obituary about Stanley Lewis, having bequeathed some of his will to the Trust, having loved exploring their wonderful gardens and properties throughout his life. His nephew having written his obituary, explaining Stanley had never married, and in his opinion, never really grown up. It began with his early education, through to secondary school, where he had excelled in nothing more than woodwork and history. Later came a stint as a pub landlord, not without incident! After returning to a more conventional career, he had enjoyed his holidays exploring our country's canal network, stopping off to visit many of the National Trust properties, always preferring to stay aboard his beloved barge. Leaving me wondering, as to who would write what about me!

The guy sat next to his wife reading the paper was just beginning to doze off when the nurse called him, leaving two free spaces. My attention is drawn outside to an open space, a neglected courtyard between buildings, realising I could have transformed it whilst waiting for my appointment, they could consider it as therapy, it would certainly be more stimulating than sitting here for so long. Within moments the remaining seats were occupied, one by a younger guy resembling a student or possibly a manual worker; his jeans looking as though they'd never actually been washed in a long time, if ever! The other seat being occupied by another dishevelled male, a little older this time, unable to remain quiet, complaining about the choice of music being played on the radio, currently 'Bananarama', after being informed, for what seemed like the fourth time, of their recent comeback. Despite the man's clothes resembling the younger guy's, his boots were remarkably clean! I kept my head down, avoiding eye contact, and feeling compelled to share my story with complete strangers. He continues informing us all, as well as the guy opposite, that he didn't watch television or read newspapers, only realising Theresa May was Prime Minister the other day! Perhaps the old magazines may be of interest after all!

Jim whispers quietly in my ear, informing me that he's going to move the car, having only parked for two hours on the road outside. The guy with the elongated face, highlighted with a goatee beard, sat minding his own business next to the window, is perhaps relieved to be the next one called. That just left the man we now knew to have dementia, who after being questioned by the older unruly guy—trying to ascertain and diagnose the cause, asks, 'Do you drink?'

'Just a glass of wine each night,' he admits, as if on trial!

The other guy in the waiting room, well dressed and undiscerning, who was by now, no doubt, probably losing the will to live, having been here since Jim and I arrived, suddenly got up and disappeared. The topic of conversation on the radio changing to verruca's and cures. One woman explaining she had had as many as a hundred at one time, on one foot! Explaining she had shared a bathroom at the time; not quite sure if this had been the cause as well as the reason for letting them multiply, but reminding me of Beth, and her infestation of nits, another childhood plague to be reckoned with. Matthew, her brother, having been quite alarmed at the prospect of having to kill these little creatures! The next caller was a mother, at her wits end, having contracted warts whilst treating her daughter's verruca. I wonder who dreams up these topics of conversation, and who would want to phone in and share such things, then I glance across and realise!

Fortunately, Jim and I had had breakfast, although now a while ago, it may well be time for afternoon tea by the time we get out!

Two and a half hours after arriving, my name was called, the nurse apologising for the wait. The news was good, nothing having changed, an appointment scheduled for the same time next year. We were free to leave, just five minutes later.

After having been inside for so long, we decide to grab some things for a picnic and enjoy the sunshine and fresh air. We even decide to celebrate with a small bottle of Champagne, not forgetting the flutes, an essential when drinking Champagne, even if they were plastic! We drive a little further out of the town, taking the time to locate the right spot. Instead of settling for the headland, we follow a track to a secluded beach, settling beside some large rocks, with a view of the escaping tide, exposing more sand. Jim pours us each a glass of Champagne.

'Good health!' he cheers, raising his glass.

'Thank you. I suppose it was worth the wait,' I acknowledge. 'Remind me to take a book next time, or a spade!'

'A spade?' Jim questions. 'What on earth for?'

'To tackle that courtyard. I spent two hours planning what to do with it!' I inform him.

'Oh!' was Jim's reply, unsure, if he'd quite understood, or believed me.

'This was a good find,' I say, continuing to tuck into my chicken leg.

'Um, I love cold chicken!' Jim agrees.

'No, I meant here,' I correct him. We may understand each other's body language, but we are still a long way off being able to finish each other's sentences!

We finish our drinks and lay down together in the warmth of the sun. In all my years, I had never made love on a beach, or come to think of it, outside! Unless you can call under canvas, outside. I'm sure it won't be our last time either! Despite having experienced many elements, we hadn't come equipped to light a fire, and as the sun had moved, so did we, heading home to the comfort of a warm bed.

Chapter 20
Treasured Memories

'So, what did you get when you were three?' Jim asks me as we drive to join Sarah and Henry to celebrate Lizzie's third birthday.

'Oh, I can't remember that far back,' I admit. 'What's your earliest memory?' I ask him.

'I was introduced to so many things on the farm from an early age, that they all just became part of everyday life. I can remember it raining once.'

'Just the once?' I ask, considering where we lived.

'Well, one time in particular,' Jim recalls. 'It never seemed to stop, there were rivers of mud. I can still smell my father's wet clothes.'

'I expect the cows were in the barn!' I quip.

'They must have been, I suppose,' Jim considers for a moment. 'Would have been cruel to leave them out in that,' he concludes, quite seriously!

'Nothing's changed much there then!' I say, catching Jim's glance.

'Just me, I suppose!'

'In what way?' I ask.

'Well, I'm a bit older for a start,' he confesses.

'So, would you change anything?' I ask him.

'Can't say as I would,' he concludes.

'Not even me?' I ask.

'Not even you!' he says, taking my hand and kissing it gently.

Jim carries in Lizzie's very large present, concealed in a beautifully wrapped box, tied up with bright pink ribbon. Whilst I carry her birthday cake I'd baked yesterday, along with an array of cakes for Kate, all decorated in the softest colours of buttercream, each topped off with a vibrant fresh flower, to tempt the taste buds and make the heart sing.

'Lizzie, Grandma and Grandad are here!' Sarah calls to her. "Grandma", it seems now, just rolls off her tongue.

'Lizzie, look! Your present's enormous!' Luke alerts her, not far behind.

'Happy birthday, Lizzie darling!' Jim wishes his granddaughter, picking her up to greet her with a kiss.

'Can I help Lizzie open her present?' Luke asks, already tearing the paper off. 'Open the box Lizzie!' he demands, unable to contain his own excitement for what could be hiding inside such an enormous cardboard box.

'Can you help me, Grandad?' Lizzie asks Jim.

Jim pulls the tape securing the box, telling Lizzie to reach inside and pull the handle.

'It's a pram!' Lizzie squeals with delight, her eyes as wide as her grin.

'That's wonderful Lizzie, isn't it?' Sarah agrees.

'Thank you, Grandad,' Lizzie says, throwing her arms around Jim's legs.

'Grandma chose it,' Jim admits.

'Thank you, Grandma,' Lizzie announces, with the same exuberance.

'Can I take Jesus for a walk?' Lizzie asks, wrapping her favourite doll in the knitted blankets I'd made, before slipping her feet into her wellies, both of which, seemed to go most places with her.

'I'll take her outside,' I volunteer, remembering how excited I'd been to push Tilly in her new pram the moment she was allowed out for the first time.

'And me!' shouts Luke, not wanting to miss out on anything this special day may hold for him, and his sister, memories they'll hold dear, maybe even treasure forever.

We joined Sarah and Henry in the garden, where Kate and Sam had joined them. The table was festooned in a long, pretty, floral cloth, with equally delicious tempting delights for us to share. Sarah had picked some delicate wild flowers, positioning them in jam jars between the plates. From the trees, she'd hung balloons and bunting.

'How pretty!' I admire, complementing Sarah on her effort.

'Thank you. Kate helped this morning. She even got cover in the café so she could be with us,' Sarah explains, whilst filling a plate each for Luke and Lizzie to enjoy, sat on a blanket under the dappled shade of the tree.

'Have you ever heard Lizzie mention Crystal?' I ask Sarah.

'No, I can't say that I have. Who is she?' Sarah asks, after a moment or two.

'She appears to be her imaginary friend,' I inform her.

'Does she mention her often?' Sarah asks, a little alarmed at the idea.

'Apparently not,' I continue. 'I've been observing her behaviour and found she only ever introduces her when either Luke is away at school, or you're not here. I think she perhaps feels a little insecure without Luke there. She is only three.'

'So do you think it's normal behaviour?' Sarah asks, a little worried now.

'I'm sure it's harmless, part of growing up, it'll pass,' I say, trying to reassure her. 'I suppose it'll help her become more assertive, a bit like role play, acting out what Luke has already taught her,' I continue. Although I can't remember any of the children I'd ever cared for introducing an imaginary friend, I could perhaps understand the reason Lizzie had. Unlike Lizzie's baby doll Jesus, who could be left behind, Crystal would always be there, just like Frank had been there for me as a child, my knight in shining armour to hold my hand.

'I can't remember Luke ever having an imaginary friend,' Sarah recalls.

'He never had an older sibling leave him, did he,' I point out.

'What did you say she calls her friend?' Sarah asks.

'Crystal,' I remind her. 'It's a beautiful name, isn't it? Almost magical!'

'I've never heard it before,' Sarah admits.

'Perhaps a character in a story book at nursery,' I suggest.

'Do you think I need to mention it to nursery?' Sarah asks.

'It might help you both understand her behaviour a little better, see if she behaves differently in there. I bet they've seen it before, you'd be surprised,' I say.

'Do you think she could possibly see someone?' Sarah suggests.

'No, I really don't think that's necessary,' I say, wrapping my arm around her to comfort her.

'Molly, I've never told anyone this before,' Sarah begins. 'Only Henry knows,' she pauses, 'Lizzie's a twin. I miscarried her brother, or sister, early in the pregnancy.'

I wrap both arms around her now, considering just how much grief she has had to endure. 'Don't worry about her, Sarah,' I implore. 'Luke understands her, and we all love her. She'll be fine. I'm sorry I've upset you today,' I say, regrettably.

'No, I'm so glad you said something. That's why I asked you to look after them,' she adds. 'I trust you.'

'See how happy she is,' I say, glancing towards Luke and Lizzie, chattering away together between mouthfuls of sandwiches. 'Crystal's probably the last thing on her mind!'

'You're probably right,' Sarah agrees.

'She'll be fine, you'll see.'

***

'Jim, do I remind you of anyone?' I ask, as we wander barefoot along the beach together before heading home.

'No,' he says, without much consideration. 'Why do you ask?'

'What was Lou like?'

'She was completely different to you,' Jim explains, dismissing any similarity. 'She was a little taller and her hair was beginning to grey, there're a few photos dotted around the house, Sarah's got a more recent one in hers, take a look for yourself next time you're there.'

'No, I mean her personality,' I ask, correcting him.

'Why do you ask?'

'It's just the way Sarah confides in me,' I tell him.

'She trusts you, that's all. Nothing to do with any resemblance to her mother,' he informs me. 'Why what's she been saying now?'

'Have you noticed Lizzie talking to someone called Crystal when we're looking after her?' I ask.

'Can't say I have,' he concludes.

'It's just I have. I think she's just a little lost when Luke's not there,' I explain.

'What does Sarah say?' he enquires.

'I think I've convinced her it's completely normal behaviour, and not to worry,' I tell him. 'Perhaps we could help her, encourage her to help care for Crocus, more responsibility for her, so she becomes more confident.'

'I suppose I could think of something,' he replies.

'Do you remember having an imaginary friend?' I ask Jim, realising how little I actually know about him.

'Not that I can remember,' he says. 'Do you think Lizzie will remember when she's our age?'

'No, I don't suppose she'll even care,' I admit. 'We'll have to keep baby Jesus though!' I say, remembering all the things Alice had kept to remind her of Frank. Even the same Shakespeare play I'd kept, though I imagine it held different memories for her than it had for either myself or Frank. Shakespeare himself having had a very wild and vivid imagination. Frank and I had recited his words of love to each other that often, we could have belonged to the local amateur dramatic group. Although, spoken with passion, they were his words, not ours.

Chapter 21
Mary's Story

It was a beautiful afternoon, perfect for enjoying outside. Grace and I were sat around a table outside a beautiful old country house hotel admiring the view across the lake, whilst waiting to meet someone very special. Whilst Grace had been sorting through her father's belongings she had come across a letter; it had been sent from Frank's natural mother, many years ago. Unable to supress her curiosity, Grace had contacted Mary, eager to find out her story. As far as either of us were aware, Frank had been told of his adoption as soon as he could understand, but that was all. As far as he had been concerned, Alice had been the only mother he had ever known or needed. Grace had already explained to Mary, that sadly, Frank had now passed away, but would love to meet her for herself, and understand her story, after all, she was her grandmother, bringing me along to fill in any gaps, having known him as a child.

'Do you think we'll recognise her?' Grace asks, looking around.

'He could have looked like his father,' I suggest.

'I never considered that.' Grace concludes.

'Maybe this is her,' I say, as a woman a little older than myself turned the corner, catching my eye.

'She's far too young, and looks nothing at all like Dad!' Grace exclaims. 'I keep imagining I'm going to see Grandma, if I'm honest. Everyone says I look like Dad, but I've never considered he couldn't have looked like Grandma, have you?'

'I don't suppose I had,' I reply, as the lady approaches us. I stand up and greet her, 'Hello, I'm Molly. This is Frank's daughter Grace.'

'Hello, I'm Mary,' she replies, sitting opposite us.

'Thank you for agreeing to see us,' Grace begins.

'It's my pleasure,' Mary says. 'It was wonderful to hear from you, especially after all this time. I never gave up hope, never moved, just in case,' she admits.

'I'm sorry you never got to meet Frank,' I tell her. 'He was a wonderful person.' I almost say she'd be proud of him, but stop myself, wondering if it was appropriate. 'Did Grace explain I grew up with Frank?' I ask.

'Yes, she did, my dear. Perhaps you can fill me in a little more,' Mary asks.

'Well, where do I begin,' I wonder. 'I feel I have always known Frank, like I said, we grew up together, saw each other every day. We lived beside a river, it became our playground as we got older. I suppose we were inseparable. Perhaps I could take you there one day,' I suggest, 'show you.'

'I'd like that,' Mary says, 'but, carry on.'

'He was very happy as a child; his parents were happy and supportive. I actually spent more time in and around his house, than my own,' I consider. 'I suppose it was idyllic. Neither of us had brothers or sisters, just each other. Frank was a year older than me, we'd walk to and from school together.' I consider Lizzie for a moment, and how she must miss Luke, the same way I had missed Frank when he'd started secondary school without me.

'I'm glad he wasn't lonely,' Mary says.

'Did you have any more children?' Grace asks.

'Yes, another son and two daughters,' she tells us.

'With my dad's father?' Grace asks.

'No, I married someone else several years later,' she informs us.

'Did you love Frank's father?' Grace continues.

'I thought I did, but all that disappeared when I discovered I was pregnant and had to face my parents,' Mary explains. 'What you have to understand is, it was very different when I was growing up, it's hard to imagine just how much things have changed in my lifetime. I was brought up to be an obedient Catholic girl, who didn't ask questions, I just did as I was told, whether I agreed or not.'

'Surely, the right Christian thing would have been for your parents to support you,' Grace considers.

'Not then, I'm afraid,' Mary explains. 'I was made to feel as though I'd brought shame on the family.'

'Did you consider keeping him?' Grace asks.

'It never crossed my mind,' Mary says. 'Like I said, I did as I was told.'

'Even after you'd given birth?' Grace continues.

'I think I'd resigned myself by then,' Mary says.

'So how old was my dad when you left him?' Grace asks, now in full flow.

'Just ten days old. My parents collected me from the hospital and drove me somewhere, whilst I cradled him for the last time, as he slept in my arms in the back of the car,' Mary recalls, with tears in her eyes. 'My mother stood beside me, whilst I handed him over to a complete stranger. Then I walked away, back to the car where my dad was waiting to take us home.'

'How old were you, when you had my dad?' Grace continues.

'I'd just turned sixteen,' Mary answers.

'Did the father know?' Grace questions, unable to stop.

'No, it was kept from him. I was never allowed to see him again,' Mary says.

'So, he never knew!' Grace says, astonished. 'Didn't he ever come looking for you?'

'Not that I recall,' Mary says. 'My parents wouldn't have entertained him anyhow. He wouldn't have come back.'

'And you never told him?' Grace asks.

'No, he'd moved on with another girl, when I eventually saw him again,' Mary tells us.

'If only he'd known,' Grace sighs.

I call the waiter over. 'Can we order some drinks?' I enquire.

'Of course, madam. What can I get you all?' he asks.

While we wait, I open the photo album I'd recently acquired from Grace, talking Mary through the individual photographs, even recalling some memories with great affection. I'd also chosen a few and copied them, placing them in a small album for Mary to keep.

'Thank you Molly, that's so thoughtful of you,' she says, appreciatively.

I can't help but feel sad, that this is all she has to show for the baby she bore.

'So, what happened once you'd given my dad away?' Grace continues her interrogation, in her remarkably insensitive manner, whilst trying to comprehend the full story. I'm beginning to think she would make a wonderful detective.

'That was it, as far as my parents were concerned, it was over. It was never mentioned again, and I was told to forget about it, pretend it never happened.'

'But obviously, you didn't,' Grace determines.

'No, I've kept it to myself. I never even told my husband or children,' Mary confides.

'Really!' Grace asks, surprised.

'How do you begin to tell your children, that you gave their brother away?' Mary asks.

'I'd learnt to live with it, although I could never forgive myself,' Mary tells us. 'I tried to keep the few memories I had alive: his beautiful blue eyes, his jet-black hair, his sweet smell, the way he curled up in my arms when I cradled him. I'd examined every little finger and toe, every crease of his perfectly formed little body. I'd look at new babies, out and about, consider if they were my Frank. I thought of him the day he would have started school, I even waited outside the school with the other mothers at home time, hoping to catch a glimpse of him. I remember hearing a mother shout the name Frank once, instinctively turning, expecting to see him standing there. Every year on his birthday I went to church, said a prayer and lit a candle for him. I knew he was out there somewhere, but I couldn't find him.'

'So, why did you call him Frank?' I ask.

'Francis was the name I remember his father had chosen for his own confirmation name,' Mary tells us.

'So, what was his full name?' Grace asks.

'Andrew Christopher Francis Barlow,' Mary informs us.

I felt for Mary, her suffering and heartache. I may not have had a baby of my own, but that might be preferable to what she has had to endure. I continue to fill Mary in on more recent times spent with Frank, his size ten feet, his beautiful broad smile, how he'd loved to spend time painting. Then more recently, his courage in adversity. Apologising for his ignorance and loss of consideration for her feelings, assuring her he'd had a very happy childhood and had been loved, and in his defence, hadn't known anything else.

'How sad you didn't get to meet him,' I say to Mary.

'I suppose I did forfeit the right,' Mary says. 'I'm so glad things eventually worked out so you could be together again, and that he wasn't alone at the end.'

'I took good care of him,' I assure her.

'Thank you, both of you. It was lovely to meet you both,' Mary concludes.

'Don't hesitate to contact us again, should you wish,' I tell her, before we part company.

Grace and I head back to her house for a well-deserved cup of tea.

'Poor woman,' I say, unable to fully comprehend how Mary must feel.

'But, like she said, she forfeited any right, the moment she agreed to give him away. She perhaps should've put up a fight,' Grace says.

'I really don't think it would have made any difference to the outcome,' I admit.

'Her parents should have considered her feelings, supported her, respected her decision if she had wanted to keep him. After all, he was their grandson,' Grace explains. 'I don't think I could ever behave like they did, I would never forgive myself.'

'Why did you ask for the father's full name? You don't intend finding him?' I ask. 'You would have to think carefully first before you did,' I explain. 'Remember as far as we know, he has no idea about any of this. You have to consider the consequences it might have.'

'Did Mary?' Grace asks. 'She was only interested in satisfying her own curiosity. I would only be doing the same. It is my grandfather we're talking about, remember.'

'Just think before you do anything,' I advise. 'Don't rush in.'

'Don't worry, I will,' she assures me.

Whilst Grace gives the children their tea, I ring Jim, informing him of my desire to return home.

'I'm glad,' Jim says, 'I can't wait either. I'll meet you off the train and have a hot meal waiting in the oven for you. It won't be long now.'

'What do you think about a hen for Lizzie?' Jim asks. 'I just think Crocus is a bit of a handful for little Lizzie.'

'Sounds a good idea,' I agree. 'She could help choose one,' I suggest, 'and I could certainly use a few more eggs. Perhaps I could have a few of my own,' I consider.

'I'll look into it,' Jim says. 'We could keep them here on the farm.'

'We'll talk about it tomorrow,' I assure him, before wishing him a good night.

Chapter 22
May Day Madness

The sun was shining, and the streets were alive with colour, little girls dressed in their pretty floral summer dresses and bandsmen in their purple jackets, adorned with twisted gold braid and shining buttons. Bunting hung between the cottages lining the street, all freshly washed with paint in celebration of the return of spring, even the pots on the gravestones had been filled with fresh flowers, including Frank's. The village hall was decked with floral bunting, and buckets of flowers greeted you outside the door. Inside were a selection of home baked cakes that the local women had contributed, that I had come to help sell, not that they needed any help! Everyone had gone to a lot of effort, although, the lemon drizzle cake I noticed, suspiciously resembled the batch displayed in the bakery window I'd passed on the way down. As well as volunteering, I'd baked an extra batch of cupcakes, decorating them with fresh edible flowers. I'd also baked some little gingerbread men, giving these chocolate features and coloured buttons on their imaginary clothes. Considering, if like in Hans Kristian Anderson's story, the children would notice.

In the other room, were a variety of stalls, one selling raffle tickets for a selection of prizes, including a meal for two at Kelvin's, a bouquet of flowers donated by Lyndsey, plus the usual lavender bath salts and other unwanted gifts. The tombola being even more of a lucky dip, with prizes usually ranging from tinned puddings and pineapple chunks, usually approaching their sell by dates, to unwanted bottled beverages, previously won at a similar event. At least everything on our stall was guaranteed fresh, if not home baked! On another stall stood plants, several of which had caught my attention. My garden already an abundance of colour, still had room for something new. It appeared we had several green fingered people in our midst. As well as donating plants they had grown, there were several gardens open to the public, which I intend to visit later in the day with Jim, and Tilly, due to arrive and join us for lunch. Tilly, keen to take advantage of the opportunity to view and gleam inspiration from other people's gardens, admiring their work, before leaving in the morning, just a short drive to her destination, for the remainder of the week, to learn more about herbaceous plants. My own gate, I'd decided would remain closed to the public. Not that I'm not proud of my little oasis, but it's not everyone, Frank included, who'd nurture nettles and dandelions alongside borage and beans. But for now, the doors had opened to the public, word had obviously got out to get here early to avoid having to bake oneself over the weekend, many I shouldn't wonder, catering for the expected and unexpected friends and family on such a lovely weekend.

Outside the sun was shining as I set off to meet Jim at Sarah's for lunch, along with everyone else, including Tilly, arriving moments later.

After lunch, we joined the crowd watching the ancient tradition of maypole dancing, one of the oldest surviving customs in the country, marking the passing of winter and the coming of summer. Luke fascinated by the plaiting and unplaiting of the coloured ribbons, Lizzie, clapping along to the music, sat on her father's shoulders.

'Don't they look beautiful?' Kate says, admiring the little girls. 'I still can't believe I'll have my own little son this time next year.'

'I thought you didn't know what sex your baby was,' I remind her.

'Oh, that was careless of me,' she says. 'Don't tell anyone, will you Molly. I told Sam I'd keep it a secret. It just slipped out!'

'Your secret's safe with me,' I tell her.

'Thank you,' she says, relieved.

'I can knit something blue now,' I admit.

'So, have you chosen him a name yet?' I ask.

'We can't decide, we've still got a bit of time though yet,' she says. 'Those cakes last week sold really quickly, they looked, and tasted amazing.'

'Oh, that's good to hear, I'll do the same again then,' I suggest.

The streets had been closed, not that there was ever much traffic through the village, but it was nice to be able to wander aimlessly along the streets.

Once the May Queen had been crowned, we all followed the brass band up the street and back down again, marching to the "Floral Dance".

The afternoons festivities over and the children in bed, Kate, having persuaded Tilly to join her, leave together to join the throng of happy people in the pub, to listen to Sam play with his band. Jim and I, having instead decided to listen to Bob play in the local brass band at a concert in church. We joined Linda, Gabriel and Eleanor who'd also decided to join us, Eleanor intrigued, after hearing all about Bob's passion. Despite the concert not yet having started, people were whispering quietly between themselves, respecting the unusual venue for a music concert. I had been told Bob played the tenor horn, different in shape to the French horn I was more familiar with, having seen it played in an orchestra alongside Poppy on her violin. Once the music started, the two old ladies behind, seemed to lose all the inhibitions they'd arrived with, becoming more and more excited as the programme unfolded.

'Oh, I do like this one!' one of them shouts above the music to her friend sitting right beside her, who was already singing along!

The conductor of a band, or orchestra, I always found fascinating to watch, each with a different level of enthusiasm for what they were asking the musicians to perform; a spectacle in their own right. This evening, the gentleman responsible didn't disappoint, beginning almost gracefully, not unlike a ballerina, poised on his toes, the music dictating his lyrical expression. Only, unlike a ballerina, his clothes somewhat restricting his movements, his short jacket rising every time he lifted his baton, emphasising his poor choice of underwear! Each time the conductor turned to us to introduce the next piece, the young euphonium player would make eyes at one of the female cornet players opposite, either thinking our attention would be diverted, or that love is truly blind!

More cake had been baked and served with a cup at tea at the interval, the band especially seemed grateful for, though I did wonder what the consequences might be, when I noticed one of them tucking into a caramel slice! Eleanor, who'd been unaware of the other entertainment on offer this evening, decided we should extend our evening out and gate crash the festivities up the road, once the band had finished their programme.

'What dressed like this?' Bob questions.

'Just take your jacket and tie off,' Eleanor tells him.

'I could certainly do with a drink!' he replies.

'So, you'll come?' Eleanor declares.

'Oh, I suppose so!'

'Don't sound too enthusiastic,' Jim adds.

'Just don't blame me if your post's late in the morning,' Bob sighs.

'No one'll notice anyway, we'll all be at work,' Eleanor says.

'Not all of us,' I hasten to add.

'I imagine you two will still be in bed,' Eleanor says.

'Let's not!' Gabriel quips.

'Isn't that Judith?' Eleanor asks, looking towards the door.

'So it is,' I say.

'Got to go!' Bob announces, as the band start to take their places for the second half.

I catch Michael's eye as they pass on the way back to their seats. 'Hi Michael, we've all decided to walk up to the pub for a drink after the concert if you and Judith would like to join us. Jim's son's playing there with his band.'

'Sounds great, we'll catch you later,' he says, before being hurried back into his seat by his wife.

The band began the second half of the concert with "What a Wonderful World". The first verse sung from the pew behind, after she'd told her companion, and everyone else, that she'd wrapped up some cake to have with her bedtime coco later!

'You may as well,' her friend replied, now too, forgetting where she was!

The band finished with a resounding medley of music from the "Pirates of the Caribbean". The duet behind, either mesmerised or asleep by now, were upstaged by the young boy on the opposite isle, directly in front of the guy on drums, who'd decided to lose himself one last time in beating his imaginary sticks to a completely different beat. Fortunately, all credit to the musician, who'd somehow managed to avoid this distraction, deserving the final applause, which alerted the old dear behind to advise everyone in earshot, that if we clapped loud enough, the band would normally provide an encore. The band obliged, to everyone's delight, concluding with the "Floral Dance".

Despite not having anything other than a cup of tea, we all managed to march in quick succession up the street with our imaginary instruments, mainly trombones, following Bob, reminding me of the Pied Piper! Michael and Judith who had followed us at a distance, silently up the hill, declined the open invitation to more merriment, once they'd eventually caught us up outside the pub, deciding to carry on up the street to where they'd left their car. Michael, looking a little disappointed, summoned by his wife, unable to join his friends.

'Early night for you!' Gabriel shouts after them.

The evening continued with more great music, singing and dancing, plenty of alcohol and even Bob, unable to resist a good night out.

Tilly, it seemed, had made friends with Guy, the spark between them obvious, even from across the room, Sam and Kate had obviously being playing Cupid!

'Hi Molly!' Tilly shouts above the music. 'I didn't see you arrive. You kept this quiet, didn't you?'

'They're not bad, are they?' I say. 'Have you met Sam's friends?' I ask.

'Yes, Guy said he's going to take me coasteering next weekend when I'm back,' Tilly tells me.

'So, should I expect to see you again?' I ask.

'Maybe, but Kate said I'd be welcome to stay at theirs next weekend, if that's all right with you?' she asks.

'That's fine by me,' I tell her. 'Perhaps makes more sense.' I figure. 'I don't suppose you're coming back with us yet then.'

'Is that all right?' Tilly enquires.

'Of course, you don't need my permission anymore,' I remind her. 'You've got a key.'

'Yes, thanks Molly,' she says, giving me a kiss. 'Jim's lovely by the way!'

'Goodnight Tilly,' I say, as Jim and I leave.

It wasn't long before I next heard from Grace. The impulsive soul she is, not at all like her father, hadn't considered the implications before contacting Andrew Barlow, informing him of what she had learnt, whilst I'm still trying to get my head around my own discovery. It appeared Andrew hadn't taken long either in replying to Grace, asking her never to contact him again.

Undefeated, and after a fresh discovery, she asks for my advice.

'I've just been talking to Sophie. She was telling me about the new couple in grandma's house,' Grace informs me over the phone. 'She mentioned their surname's Barlow.'

'Wasn't that the name of Frank's father?' I ask.

'Yes, exactly!' Grace says. 'They could be my cousins,' she continues, 'living in their uncle's house!'

'I suppose that's a possibility,' I consider, 'or it could just be a coincidence!'

'If their grandfather was to visit them, he'd be sat in the same living room, looking out of the same kitchen window his own son had.' Grace realises, remaining quiet, perhaps allowing her thoughts to catch up with her recent discovery.

'This is what happens when you start digging up the past. Sometimes it's best left there,' I tell her, reminded of my own discovery, wondering if I'd have perhaps preferred to have remained in the dark.

'But, isn't it better we know?' Grace asks.

'Not always,' I say.

'Don't you want to know?'

'I just can't help wondering where all this might lead, what damage it might do,' I explain. 'You said yourself, Andrew wasn't too pleased, and what about Mary? Her family have no idea.'

'They might be interested to discover the connection,' Grace suggests.

'But you have to respect their privacy. You can't just go knocking on their door,' I explain, realising Grace might be inclined to do just that.

'I could get to know them, find out if they're who I think they are,' Grace says.

'I suggest you let the dust settle before you do anything,' I advise her, hoping she'll heed my advice this time. 'I imagine it must have come as an enormous shock to Andrew. Let him get used to the idea, he may just change his mind.'

'Do you think so?' Grace asks, enthusiastically.

'It's quite possible. It's a lot for him to take in,' I remind her.

'I hope you're right,' she says. 'Thanks Molly, I knew you'd know what to do.'

Jim found me on the rocks, a favourite place of mine to sit and think, often just letting the waves crash and spill across the stones below, easing my mind, my thoughts erased with each retreating wave.

'What's on your mind Molly?' Jim asks, sitting down beside me.

'Oh, I've just been talking to Grace,' I tell him, explaining what she'd gone and done, and how it'd made me think of my own history. Jim, obviously realising I must have been sat here a while, the waves now splashing at our feet, suggests we retreat whilst we still have the opportunity.

'You're cold,' Jim says, taking my hand.

'Am I?' I ask, not having noticed.

'Let's get you home,' he suggests. 'I expect you could do with a hot drink.'

'I suppose,' I admit, begrudgingly.

Jim guides me home, fuels the stove and fills the kettle. Leaving it to boil, he joins me on the sofa, wrapping his arm around me. He kisses me tenderly on my cheek before retreating into the kitchen, returning with a steaming mug of camomile tea and a packet of chocolate biscuits.

'Thank you,' I tell him, 'I'm so lucky to have you.'

'I love you Molly,' he tells me.

'And I love you,' I reply.

Chapter 23
Grief and Sadness

Despite having given Jim a key to my house, he still insisted on ringing the bell rather than letting himself in, until this evening. He had already tried phoning me when I had failed to answer the door, expecting me ready and waiting to go and look after the children.

'Molly, wake up!' he nudged me, as I lay sleeping on the sofa. 'Molly, are you alright?' he asks, sounding alarmed. 'Had you forgotten, we're meant to be looking after the children tonight?'

'Oh, I'm sorry Frank, I'd completely forgotten. I must have nodded off. I can meet you there if you want to go ahead,' I suggest.

'No, I'll go on my own, you get an early night,' he says.

'Are you sure? It won't take me long to get ready.'

'No, honestly, an early night will do you good, I'll stay there tonight so I won't disturb you. I'll call you in the morning,' he says, leaving me to rest.

'Hi Dad! Where's Molly?' Sarah asks, opening the door.

'I left her resting, she seems tired,' Jim informs his daughter.

'Is she all right?'

'Yes, just tired, I think.'

'I wanted to talk to you on your own anyway,' Sarah says. 'Have you noticed anything odd about Molly's behaviour recently?'

'How do you mean?'

'Well, yesterday, when I was taking the children down to the beach, I noticed her sitting on the ground next to Frank's grave,' she says.

'Oh, don't worry about that,' Jim informs her. 'I know she still visits him.'

'No Dad, she was still sitting there when we returned!' Sarah replies, concern in her voice. 'I sent the children over to alert her, she seemed miles away and she hadn't left any flowers.'

'Did you leave her there?' Jim asks.

'No, we invited her back with us.'

'How was she?'

'A little distant,' Sarah says. 'Can't quite put my finger on it.'

'Now you come to mention it, I have noticed she's not quite herself recently. She seems preoccupied, other things on her mind, and just before, she called me Frank!' Jim says. 'She hasn't been sleeping too well recently, some nights she lies tossing and turning, or wakes from a bad dream. Perhaps it's just tiredness,' he suggests.

'But why's she not sleeping?' Sarah asks. 'You haven't upset her?'

'No, not that I'm aware of,' Jim answers. 'What do you propose I do?'

'Talk to her,' Sarah suggests, 'and keep a close eye on her.'

The following morning, I decided to go and meet Jim, and apologise to Sarah.

'Hi Molly!' Sarah says, answering the door, still in her pyjamas. 'You're up early.'

'Yes, I couldn't sleep,' I say, realising the house is unusually quiet. 'Where is everyone?'

'They're all still in bed!' Sarah informs me.

'Come in the kitchen, Molly, I'll make us some coffee,' she says, closing the door. 'How are you?'

'Oh, all right, a little tired maybe,' I reply. 'I haven't been sleeping too well recently.'

'I thought you weren't quite yourself,' Sarah comments.

'Do you ever feel like you're floating outside your body, as though you're not quite in control of what's happening, or what you're doing?' I ask.

'As though it's happening to someone else?' Sarah asks, trying to understand.

'Yes, you know what I mean?'

'No, not really,' she replies.

'Well, that's how I feel,' I say.

'Has Dad done something to upset you?' Sarah asks. 'He can be insensitive sometimes, without even realising it.'

'No, not at all,' I continue. 'Why do you ask?'

'I think he's a little worried about you, we both are.'

'What's he been saying?' I ask, a little shocked.

'Just that you don't seem your normal self, that's all.'

The days progressed in much the same vain as usual, until Jim had discussed his concerns with Sophie over the phone whilst I was out delivering cakes to Kate. Then on my return, Jim sat me down.

'Molly, Sophie rang whilst you were out,' he said.

'Did you tell her I'd ring her back?' I ask.

'Not exactly,' Jim says, inviting me to sit beside him on the sofa.

'Is she alright?' I ask, a little worried.

'Yes, she's fine,' Jim reassures me. 'It's you we're concerned about.'

'Why?' I ask, though conscious I've been causing concern.

'You've not been yourself just recently,' Jim continues. 'Do you think you need a break?'

'What a holiday?' I ask.

'Sophie suggested you go and stay with her for a while,' Jim says.

'Are you trying to get rid of me?'

'No, I'm trying to help you Molly. I love you,' he tells me. 'I think you need time to clear your head, make sense of everything that's happened. You can't do that with me around.'

'But I love you,' I tell him.

'I love you too Molly, but you're not yourself. I don't want to lose you,' Jim says. 'Go and spend some time with Sophie, it'll do you good.'

'Do you really think so?' I ask, realising what he'd just said.

'Give her a call while I'm out,' he says, realising I would listen to Sophie and at a loss as to what else to do. Sophie as ever knew exactly what to say, and before long had persuaded me to go and stay with her to recharge my batteries.

Jim drove me the four hundred miles to Sophie's house, still uncomfortable with the decision that had been made on my behalf, feeling like an evacuee, being sent away for my own safety. I hadn't packed for every eventuality, leaving my heels at home, not anticipating any nights out, instead choosing socks and walking boots for walks along the river. Though all was not lost, ensuring matching underwear was high on my list, along with my favourite ring, a good book and a picture of Frank, afraid I might just forget his smile, and my phone to talk to Jim.

Jim stayed overnight, setting of home again, after enjoying a lazy breakfast shared together. Perhaps he had been right, a change might just be what I needed. The sun was shining as I waved goodbye to Jim; for how long, nobody knew.

A few days later and still unsettled, I call Jim, trying to explain how I feel.

'I don't know if being here is helping. It just brings memories of Frank flooding back,' I explain. 'I thought I'd drawn a line under all that.'

'Maybe you just need to embrace it,' Jim suggests.

'But I've moved on since then. I've built a new life with you now,' I say.

'Yes, but perhaps too quickly,' Jim considers.

'Well it's too late now, we can hardly turn the clock back, can we?' I point out.

'No, I realise that,' he says. 'Just give it time.'

'Are you implying I've acted inappropriately. Disrespected Frank's memory?' I ask, considering everything.

'No, I'm not,' Jim replies.

'Perhaps I should be wearing black!' I suggest. 'Declined your advances.'

'No, perhaps I should have been more sensitive, not taken advantage of your vulnerability,' Jim says.

'I'm going to go now,' I say. 'This isn't helping me at all. I thought you were meant to be my friend. I thought I could trust you.'

'I still am, and you can,' he tells me.

'Bye Jim. I'd rather you didn't call me again. You've achieved what you set out to do,' I say.

'What do you mean by that?' he asks.

'Well, like I said earlier, I didn't choose to come here. It was your idea, not mine,' I remind him. 'Who do you think you are making a decision like that? You're not my psychiatrist, not that I have one, even need one. Well, not until I got involved with you,' I hasten to add.

'I'm sorry you feel I'm to blame,' Jim says.

'You've now made it impossible for me to return,' I continue, now upset and angry. 'I've built my life around your family, who, by the way, live on my own doorstep, call me Grandma. You've obliterated all memory of Frank,' I conclude, suddenly reminded of him.

'I never meant to Molly,' Jim says.

'But the fact is, you have. Goodnight Jim.'

Chapter 24
Grief Gone Wrong

Jim, unsure even as to whether Molly will return, devotes his time and attention to his herd, whilst continuing to care for his grandchildren alone, respecting Molly's decision and not calling her. He'd agreed to help Kate's mum, Angela, collect the pram, now in store and having room in his Land Rover.

'Kate tells me you've been experiencing a few problems with Molly,' Angela begins, as they arrive home.

'Well, it appears she might be right. I haven't heard from her in a while and she's refusing to talk to me,' Jim confides.

'Has she had a breakdown?' Angela enquires.

'I suppose, of sorts,' Jim considers.

'You weren't to know, I suppose it takes time to find these things out,' Angela says.

'Let me help you upstairs with those things. I'll put them in Kate's room, she'll be so excited,' Angela insists, taking a handful of bags from Jim.

'Thank you,' Jim says.

'I'll just slip my shoes off,' she says, before reaching the stairs, letting the straps on her dress slip seductively from her shoulders, then, turning towards him, their lips meet in a frenzied kiss. Jim, apparently not as oblivious to a woman's advances as Molly had imagined.

Without wasting any time, she helps him out of his clothes, encouraging his participation in her long-awaited fantasy. Jim, leading her across the landing, now fully aroused and ready to lose himself, along with all thoughts of Molly.

Angela didn't wait long before seizing another opportunity to see Jim, calling round, knowing Sam and Kate would both be out at an antenatal class, telling Jim she had completely forgotten, Jim inviting her in, suggesting she stay until they get back, Angela, brushing past him in her low-cut blouse, her cleavage sprinkled with some seductive scent, more sophisticated than Molly's organic blend of essential oils, taller in height in her heels, not a blonde hair out of place, her make up applied with precision, and her nails perfectly polished. Not a hint of Molly to remind him. Her eyes glancing upstairs as they reach the hallway. Jim, immediately taking her in his arms, kissing her, unable to resist, leading her upstairs and into his room once more.

The following morning, Jim arrived as planned, pulling up in front of Angela's very imposing residence, just as he had done with Molly, as guests at his son's wedding reception. Not that he'd want to recall that today. As always, he'd just stepped out of the shower, ever conscious to maintain his reputation and appeal. Angela was waiting at the door, keeping him focused, allaying any fears he might have.

'Good morning James,' she greets him, preferring to give him his full title, which he didn't mind, in fact, found rather attractive.

'You look ravishing!' he says, taking her in his arms.

'I'm glad you think so,' she replies, pleased she'd achieved the desired effect, kissing him in return and leading him inside. 'We've got the entire house at our disposal, but I thought I'd show you the master suite,' she says, leading him up the stairs, into an already prepared bedroom, a bottle of Champagne chilling in an ice bucket.

'Shall we partake?' she says, pouring them each a glass. 'Cheers!' she says, as they both take a sip. Angela slowly slipping out of her clothes in front of him.

'Now your turn, James. Let me help you,' she offers, as he raises his arms to undo his cuffs, languishing in her display of affection.

They remained where they were for the rest of the morning, Jim eventually realising he was in no fit state to drive home, ordered himself a taxi, returning that evening to collect his vehicle, only to remain there overnight, waking up next to a very attractive woman who had introduced him to the morning with a long and passionate kiss. Jim beginning to wonder why he had ever ignored her advances. She certainly knew how to captivate a man.

'How long is your husband away for?' Jim asks.

'All week!'

'Aren't we the lucky ones,' he smiles.

'It certainly feels that way from where I'm lying!' she confesses.

'I can't think of anywhere I'd rather be,' Jim decides, rolling over and kissing her again.

Jim left before lunch, heading home, if only to get some sleep, feeling deprived in that department, informing her he'd be back tomorrow.

'Until then!' Angela agreed, giving him a kiss.

Meanwhile, I was actually enjoying time spent with Sophie, helping her in the garden, shelling peas and beans to cook with freshly dug potatoes, and making jam with the abundance of soft fruit. When I wasn't busy, I would simply relax with my book, my senses soothed by the subtle fragrance and gentle bird song, in her little corner of paradise.

'This is perfect Sophie, thank you for letting me stay,' I tell her, ever grateful for her love and affection.

'It's lovely to have you here, Molly. It's my pleasure,' Sophie replies.

'I do love him,' I tell her.

'I know you do. You just need time to yourself to process everything. I've explained to Grace, she's not to go bothering our new neighbours, to just accept what happened. You've not to go getting upset about all that business, Frank was right to leave it. It all happened a long time ago and he never suffered because of it, neither has Grace, so let that be the end of it.'

I decided to call Sarah to see how they all were, unready to call Jim, just yet.

'Hi Molly, how are you?' she asks.

'Not quite ready to come home yet,' I tell her. 'How are you?'

'We're all fine. The children were just talking about you this morning over breakfast.'

'That's nice to know,' I consider, realising they could have quite easily accepted my absence and forgotten about me by now. 'How's your dad?' I ask.

'Has he not called you yet?'

'No, I haven't heard anything from him,' I explain. 'Though we did have words. I'm afraid I might have seemed ungrateful. I realise now, he was just concerned and trying to help me, but I perhaps said some things I shouldn't have.'

'Oh, don't worry yourself about that Molly, he'll understand. Wait till you get back, it'll all sort itself out. I hardly see him these days, he'll be busying himself with the herd,' Sarah explains.

'Well, at least he's got them to occupy him,' I say, realising he won't be lonely.

'You take care Molly. I'll tell Dad you called,' she says.

Chapter 25
Home Is Where the Heart Is

I hadn't in fact heard anything more from Jim whilst I'd been away. I'd resisted calling him, worried I'd just upset things. I had begun to realise, that it had been me who had invited him into my life, encouraged him to share my bed, without a second thought for Frank, unable to comprehend the consequences. It had been several days after returning home, that I'd bumped into him.

'Grandma!' I heard a familiar little voice behind me.
'Hello Lizzie,' I say, turning around.
'Where've you been?' she asks.
'I've been visiting a friend,' I explain.
'When did you get back?' Jim asks.
'A few days ago,' I tell him.
'And you didn't think to tell me?' he says.
'I didn't hear from you once, the whole time I was away,' I remind him.
'I thought that was what you wanted.'
'Well I'm back now.'
'How are you?' he asks.
'A lot better, thank you. I'm sorry for some of the things I said.'
'No, I understand,' he says.
'Where are you going Lizzie?' I ask.
'To the beach. Will you come with us Grandma?' she asks.
'I'd like that,' I tell her. 'If that's all right with Grandad?' I ask, looking at Jim for a reaction.
'Fine by me,' he agrees.
'So, tell me, how've you been?' I ask Jim.
'Fine!'

'I missed you,' I tell him. Jim falling silent, as we continue on our way.

'Are we going to paddle?' I ask Lizzie, taking off my sandals as we arrive at the beach.

'I've missed you Molly,' Jim eventually says, as though nothing has happened.

'Come and join us then,' I invite him, as I take Lizzie's hand.

'How've you been sleeping?' Jim asks.

'Like a child!' I tell him, remembering how peaceful it had been by the river. 'But I've missed you since I've been back,' I comment, hoping he might suggest joining me tonight.

'I've got a new hen!' Lizzie interrupts, 'and a kitten!'

'Oh, wonderful!' I reply. 'Can I come and look?' I ask.

'Can we go and show her, Grandad?' she asks.

'I suppose,' Jim says, a little reluctantly, as Lizzie runs ahead.

'When did this all happen?' I ask.

'Whilst you've been away,' Jim says, as I realise life waits for no man.

'How's Luke?' I ask.

'Fine!'

'So what else have I missed?'

'His sport's day,' he tells me.

'Oh, that's a pity,' I say, wishing I'd been there.

'Tell me, how did he do?' I ask. Jim seemingly reluctant to volunteer any information.

'He won the running race,' he informs me.

'Oh, that's wonderful!' I say. 'I bet he was thrilled. I wish I'd been there.'

We tiptoe into Lizzie's house, having been warned Chloe might be sleeping.

'She's only a kitten, she still sleeps a lot,' Lizzie explains, as we find her asleep on a pink blanket, in a little cardboard box.

'Shall we leave her to sleep?' I suggest. 'Does your new hen lay lots of eggs?' I ask.

'Yes, do you want to go and see?' Lizzie asks.

'Yes, I'd like that,' I tell her. 'Are there any eggs I can have to bake with?' I ask, noticing a bowlful in the kitchen. 'I said I'd bake for Kate.'

'When did you see her?' Jim asks, suddenly alert.

'I didn't, I spoke to her on the phone this morning,' I say.

'Take some of these, we collected them earlier,' Jim says.

'Thank you,' I say, appreciating how fresh they are.

'Well, I should get back I suppose, and get cracking!' I say, hoping for a response.

'Right!' was all Jim managed to say.

'Well, it was nice seeing you,' I tell them.

'Yes, likewise,' Jim replies, obviously still upset.

I wandered home, alone with my own thoughts, considering how much I must have hurt Jim. I immersed myself in baking, hoping Jim might call, hold me in his arms and make everything right between us. He did in fact call on his way back home, to see if I wanted him to take the cakes I'd baked for Kate.

'I'll come with you,' I suggest, 'I was just about to leave myself.'

'You don't need to do that,' he says.

'But I'd like to see her. I've got some things I've knitted for the baby that I'd like to give her,' I explain.

'I can do that,' Jim says.

'Why don't you want me to come?' I ask. At which point he falls silent.

'I can go on my own if you'd prefer?' I say.

'No, we'll go together,' Jim says, holding the tin of cakes as I lock the door.

I assume Kate's mum is visiting, as her car is outside the farmhouse when we arrive.

'I expect we're going to have to get used to seeing her around more, especially once the baby's arrived,' I tell Jim.

'I hadn't considered that,' he says.

'Never mind,' I remind him, 'there's always mine!'

'Why, hello James!' Angela exclaims as we arrive inside. 'Now I know why I haven't seen much of you recently.'

'Hi!' I announce, leaving the cakes in the kitchen and handing Kate a bag containing the items I'd knitted.

'Oh, thank you Molly!' Kate says, as she pulls out a little white cardigan and bootees for her baby. 'They're so sweet, and tiny!'

'Do babies even wear bootees these days?' Angela asks.

'Well, ours will,' Kate tells her. 'They're beautiful.'

'I'm afraid I'm no good in that department!' Angela says. 'Though I've heard it's supposed to be very therapeutic.'

'Are you staying long?' Jim asks her, a little abruptly.

'Not if I'm not welcome!' Angela replies.

'You were going anyway, Mum,' Kate adds.

'I know where I'm not wanted!' Angela says.

'I don't think he meant that!' Kate says, in Jim's defence. 'You're always welcome, Mum.'

'Goodbye James,' Angela shouts from the hallway as she leaves.

'Do you think she's been drinking?' I ask Jim, alarmed by her unusual behaviour.

'Shush, Kate's coming back,' Jim warns me.

'Sorry about that,' Kate says. 'You know what she can be like. She's gone now.'

'Don't worry,' I tell her.

'Are you two staying over?' Kate asks.

'No,' Jim answers, almost immediately.

'But now you're here,' Kate begins.

'You haven't come prepared,' Jim says, looking at me.

'You could always pack a bag and stay over at mine,' I suggest.

'I can always find you something to sleep in, and a toothbrush, then you can both stay and relax,' Kate says. 'As soon as Sam's showered, we're on our way out, we won't be back until lunchtime tomorrow.'

I look at Jim to gauge his reaction. 'No,' I say. 'I think it's best I don't. Thanks anyway Kate.' Realising it had never been Jim's intention. For some reason, I can't quite seem to comprehend him at the moment.

'Shall I call a taxi?' I ask, looking at Jim.

'No, there's no need, are you ready?' he asks.

'Whenever you are!' I say.

'Thanks for the cakes Molly, and the lovely knitting,' Kate says, giving me a hug as we leave. 'See you soon.'

The short distance home was uncomfortable and silent.

'Thank you,' I say, as Jim pulls up outside my house. 'I'll not ask you in.'

'I know where I'm not welcome!' Jim replies.

'I suggested you pack a bag,' I remind him. 'Would you like to come in?' I ask.

'I don't know,' Jim says, looking at me, as if remembering what we'd once shared.

'Well, shall I just sit here until you decide?' I ask.

'It's getting late,' Jim observes, rather negatively. Unable, it seems, to decide whether he should be returning home, or going to bed!

'I'm well aware of the time,' I tell him. 'I'm waiting for you to decide what you want to do,' I remind him.

'I'd like to kiss you Molly,' he says, leaning towards me.

'I've missed you, but I thought you might decide not to come back,' he continues.

'But this is my home!' I remind him.

'And where Frank is,' Jim finishes.

'Does that bother you?' I ask.

'No!' he snaps.

'Then why mention it?'

'I don't know, I suppose I'm trying to understand you, that's all,' he explains.

'I'll always love Frank. I thought you understood that.'

'I do,' Jim answers.

'You've obviously had time to think whilst I've been away, had second thoughts,' I remark.

'No,' Jim says, still unable to convince me otherwise.

'Well, it's certainly the impression you've been giving me,' I tell him.

'I think it's best you go home, decide what it is you do want. Goodnight Jim,' I say, opening the door and not looking back.

Jim returned home, and his evening had continued as planned, Kate and Sam had left, and Angela was sat waiting on the driveway in her car.

'What did you bring her along for?' she asks, as Jim walks over to meet her.

'I've taken her home now,' Jim says.

'I'm pleased to hear it, we don't want her spoiling our fun now, do we?' Angela says, wrapping her arms around him, before disappearing inside together.

I spent the following morning with Tilly, down for the weekend to see Guy. At least their romance was blossoming, despite the distance between them. As ever she had brought more plants and vegetables for my already bursting garden, explaining they'll just mingle, and climb if necessary!

We didn't waste any time in finding the perfect outfit for Tilly to wear for dinner with Guy's parents, knowing the perfect place to take her shopping.

'I knew I could ask you Molly,' Tilly says, almost relieved. 'You always look perfectly dressed for any occasion, always beautiful and feminine.'

'Thank you,' I say, flattered.

'I was shopping with Mum last week, but I daren't ask her for advice,' Tilly admits.

'I hope you don't mind me saying, but I think your mother needed a little help in the fashion department.'

'Tell me about it! She still hasn't improved. I'm just glad her feet are smaller than mine, or she'd be borrowing my killer heels!' she says.

'And how's Tom?' I ask.

'Enjoying every minute, or so I'm led to believe. I think he enjoys the attention she receives when they're out.'

'She is attractive,' I comment.

'Yes, that's just it, she doesn't need to dress as though she's thirty something,' Tilly explains. 'I'm afraid it's only going to get worse. She still insists on driving to work in her heels, looking like she's going on a night out!'

'Quite inappropriate, when you consider she's a health and safety officer!' I comment.

'Extremely! I just haven't the heart to tell her. That's why I can trust you. Remember the time you forbid me to wear that repulsive blouse to school on own clothes day?'

'How could I forget! Some things should definitely remain behind closed doors,' I remind her, 'or the garden gate.' Remembering an embarrassing occasion when I'd run around the front of the house to catch the postman with a parcel, in nothing other than a bikini, having been ordered to wait in for the delivery. It still makes me blush, forty years later!

'And that time I'd forgotten to change my school shoes!' Tilly recalls. 'Your face said it all!'

'You'd tell me if I dressed inappropriately?' I ask her.

'I doubt that would ever happen,' she says.

'Promise me?' I ask her.

'Promise!' she says, touching my hand. 'I do love spending time with you Molly, I always did.'

Inside the shop we rummage through the rails, well, more separate the garments carefully on either side of the chosen item we wish to consider, we are after all in an expensive boutique, rather than a high street outlet. Somewhere, I imagine Tilly's mother might shop. Still, such a pity some shop assistants aren't able to be more honest when asked for their opinion.

'What about this top?' Tilly asks.

'What would you wear it with?' I ask.

'Jeans!' she suggests.

'I thought you wanted to create the right impression, impress,' I remind her.

'True!' She says, replacing it.

Between us we chose three dresses for Tilly to try and a couple for myself.

'I do wish there were more mirrors in a changing room,' I hear Tilly squirm from the other side of the cubicle.

'Are you ready?' she asks.

'Yes, you?'

'I'm not sure?' she says, drawing back the curtain.

'I see what you mean,' I say, it isn't very flattering.

The shop assistant, or sales adviser as they are known in such an establishment, appears from around the corner. 'Doesn't she look beautiful!' she says, looking at Tilly.

'Do you think so?' Tilly asks doubtfully.

'Absolutely not!' I remind her. 'Try the next one on.'

'I love your dress,' Tilly comments, complimenting me on my choice.

'Thank you. I rather like it myself.' I decide, returning behind my curtain.

By now the sales advisor is helping a woman choose an outfit for a wedding, complimenting her choice as she steps out from behind the curtain for her approval. After a sly peek, I meet with her approval, though consider, when it comes to weddings there is more to consider than first meets the eye. First and foremost, one must never upstage the bride, believe me this has been known! Always check what colour the bridesmaids decide to wear, I say decide, as it is a woman's prerogative to change her mind! Then of course the flowers, the mother of the bride's outfit, not forgetting the groom's mother, one mustn't be mistaken for either, or worse, duplicate any element of their attire. Though finding a hat these days is difficult enough, without having the added worry of duplicating the aforesaid. Just imagine sitting opposite someone displaying the same plumage as yourself, it would be like a schoolgirl outing, something only my generation could sympathise with! Hats are one thing, and possibly jewellery, that you can go off-piste and have fun expressing yourself with, just as long as you can afford to, remembering it is only Beth on Corrie, and Pat Butcher on East Enders who can truly get away with baubles hanging from their ears!

We both manage to choose one beautiful dress each from the ones we'd tried on, walking away happy, Tilly excited for the evening ahead.

I wasn't going to let Jim prevent me attending church, so wasn't surprised to see him at the end of the pew when I arrive, late as ever! He moves along to make room for me to join them. We exchange glances and smile at each other, well we are in church! I had in fact arrived as the bells were ringing, but as it was already a warm day, I'd decided to put the roses I'd picked from the garden earlier, in the pot on Frank's grave, rather than watching them wilt as James shared his thoughts on adultery. I often wonder whether he is addressing the whole congregation, or just one individual person, who he feels needs his guidance, though it is probably only my imagination, as he is looking straight towards me! We conclude the service with Hymn number 330, before filtering outside into the sunshine.

'Molly, it's so lovely to see you here,' Sarah says, genuinely pleased to see me. 'You will join us for lunch?' she continues, assuming of course I will.

'I'd love too, if you're absolutely sure?' I ask.

'We won't take no for an answer, will we Henry?' she asks, linking arms with her husband.

'She has missed you!' Henry declares.

I smile as we walk together the short distance back to their house.

I join Sarah in the kitchen whilst it's quiet.

'How's Lizzie these days?' I ask. 'Is Crystal still making an appearance?'

'You know, I'd completely forgotten about Crystal!' She declares.

'That's a lovely photo of your mother,' I say, walking through to the table with the cutlery, recognising a beautiful image of her, displayed on the sideboard.

'Yes, it's one of my favourites. Your sadness actually taught me something,' Sarah admits. 'Helped me accept what happened. I realised I should share my memories. I want Luke and Lizzie to know all about her,' she pauses, 'she would have loved them.'

'I'm sorry I let you all down,' I say to her.

'Don't be silly Molly, we all struggle to make sense of things from time to time. You sometimes just need space to collect your thoughts, process everything. Life won't wait while you get your head round it. You have to take time out to smell the trees, watch the world go by, till you're ready to dip your toe in the water again.'

'I think you're right you know,' I tell her. 'You're a wonderful mother. Your mother would have been so proud of you.'

'I do my best!' she says.

'That was rather a strong sermon for a Sunday morning, even for James. Don't you think?' Sarah comments as we enjoy our lunch.

'Yes, I thought so too,' I agree.

Jim, it appeared, seemed quite at ease with my decision to accept Sarah's invitation, perhaps he'd reconsidered, or maybe it was just the fact we weren't alone. Either way I was made to feel very comfortable, almost at home, as if I'd never been away.

'So, do you go to church when you visit Sophie?' Sarah asks.

'Yes, though I must say the vicar there isn't quite as passionate as James,' I declare.

'Did you hear him, Dad?' Sarah asks.

'I wasn't really listening,' he admits, scraping Lizzie's plate for her.

'Where are Kate and Sam today?' I ask.

'They're having lunch with her parents before they go away for a couple of weeks, before the baby's arrival.'

'Where are they going?' I ask.

'I'm not sure actually,' Sarah says, 'but you can be sure it'll be on a par to what they have become accustomed to.'

'They do own a beautiful house,' I admit.

'I'd love to see upstairs, wouldn't you?' I say.

'Can you imagine?' Sarah adds.

'I expect we can only imagine, I suspect we're never going to get an invitation,' I say.

'We'll have to interrogate Sam, surely he'll have stayed. Though I doubt he will have appreciated the finer details,' Sarah comments.

'Listen to us, we'll be getting a lecture on the tenth commandment next week if we're not careful!' I warn her.

'Remind me, which one's that?' she asks.

'Thou shalt not covet thy neighbour's house, wife, ox or ass,' I remind her.

'What does covet mean?' Luke asks.

'It means to want something that belongs to someone else,' Sarah explains.

'Is that a sin?' he asks. 'I want a hamster, like Jake has, and Holly took baby Jesus home with her because she wanted him.'

'It's getting worse!' Henry declares. 'There'll be extra Sunday school if the Reverend James hears about this!'

'That's a little bit different,' Sarah explains. 'Lizzie let Holly borrow baby Jesus because she liked him so much and wanted to look after him.'

'But she won't give him back!' Luke informs us.

'Isn't that stealing?' Henry asks.

'Lizzie is good at caring for things, especially Chloe,' Sarah tells us, trying to change the subject.

'I'd look after a hamster if you'd let me have one!' I hear Luke mumble quietly to himself.

'What did you learn in Sunday school today?' Sarah asks.

'About a man who swallowed a fish,' Lizzie informs us.

'No, a fish who swallowed a man!' Luke corrects her.

'There was an old woman who swallowed a fly!' Henry chirps.

'Tell me more,' Sarah asks, glaring at Henry.

'She swallowed the spider to catch the fly!' Henry continues, amusing Luke.

'What happened next?' Sarah asks Lizzie, ignoring her husband.

'He didn't water his plant,' Lizzie explains.

'So, did it die?' Sarah asks.

'Yes, like Luke's sunflower,' she says.

'So, what should he have done?' Sarah continues.

'Water it!' Lizzie says.

'Why didn't the man die?' Luke asks me.

'Because God loved him and forgave him, like Mummy loves you,' I explain.

'So, if I say sorry, will she let me have a hamster?' he asks.

'How about we talk to her later,' I suggest.

'Great!' he agrees, picking up his cup.

'I've made trifle for dessert,' Sarah informs us, carrying a large glass bowl to the table. 'Do you remember this, Dad, wasn't it grandma's dish?'

'Yes, I believe it was,' Jim recalls.

'Home grown!' Sarah informs us.

'How can you grow a dish?' Luke asks.

'Not the dish itself,' Sarah laughs. 'The trifle inside!'

'You can't grow a trifle?' Luke continues.

'No, to be specific, the ingredients are produced here, the strawberries, the cream, milk and eggs,' Sarah informs us.

'Did Clover lay the eggs Mummy?' Lizzie asks proudly.

'At least one of them,' Sarah tells her.

'Well then, it must be good for us!' Henry decides.

'Delicious!' I compliment, before enjoying another spoonful and accepting an obligatory glass of sherry to accompany the already dosed dish. Luke and Lizzie had been served their own individually prepared portions, without the alcohol, which they had obviously enjoyed, managing to scrape their own dishes clean, before asking for seconds, as does Jim, along with another glass of sherry.

'Can I have some sherry too?' Luke asks.

'And me!' Lizzie adds, after quickly finishing the contents of her beaker and holding it up!

'I'm afraid not,' Sarah tells them. 'It's like communion wine, it's too strong for little children.'

'So, when I'm as old as Ben can I?' Luke asks.

'We'll see!' Sarah concludes.

'I could sleep now!' Jim informs us, as the children leave the table to go and play.

'You two go outside into the garden,' Sarah suggests to Jim and me, 'whilst it's quiet.'

'I'll help you with the washing up,' I offer, starting to stack the bowls.

'No, I insist,' Sarah says. 'Henry and I'll do it. Dad, take Molly outside,' she orders.

'This is nice,' Jim says, relaxing, as we sit together under the shade of the tree at the bottom of the garden.

Maybe I'll just have to buy a bottle of sherry, I consider!

It was the following morning when I literally bumped into Jim again as I was leaving the bakery.

'Oh hello, I didn't expect to bump into you,' Jim says.

'Who were you expecting?' I ask.

'Possibly the vicar, checking up on me!' he replies, looking down the street.

'Why, what are you guilty of?' I ask.

'Are you in a hurry?'

'Why, have you something you want to get off your chest?' I continue.

'I thought we could go for a drink, if you like,' Jim suggests.

'That would be lovely, but why not come back with me and I'll make us lunch,' I offer.

'If you're sure?' he asks.

'I'm sure,' I tell him. So happy, I want to skip home!

'I'm glad you're feeling better,' he says. 'You look really well.'

'All the better for seeing you,' I remark.

'You only saw me yesterday!' he reflects.

'But I miss you,' I tell him.

'Well we'll have to rectify that,' he says, as we climb the hill back to mine.

The days turned into weeks as we continued seeing each other, spending time looking after the children, falling asleep in each other's arms at the end of the day. Slowly but surely, falling back in love with each other, all over again.

Chapter 26
Never Judge a Book by Its Cover

Our next engagement was dinner with Eleanor, which surprised and intrigued us both. But as I had come prepared to construct a dessert, we wouldn't go completely hungry. The fact there were no alluring aromas didn't alarm us either, as we'd arrived early as requested, four-thirty to be precise.

'Come on in,' Eleanor greets us. 'It's so nice to see you again Molly.'

'And you,' I comment, following her into the kitchen with a bag of ingredients for later.

'I'll go and find Gabriel,' Jim says. 'He might be pleased to see me!'

'Don't be like that,' I tell him. 'Off you go, and take that beer.'

'How are you?' I ask Eleanor.

'Glad it's the weekend!' she sighs.

'Tough week?' I ask.

'Busy!' she explains. 'Especially now it's the school holidays.'

'Of course,' I say, not having considered the impact on a dental surgery before.

'Have you ever tried yoga?' I ask her.

'No, why?' she asks.

'It could help you relax, you should give it a try,' I suggest, as we join the guys who've already made themselves at home.

'Isn't it difficult, all those contorted positions?' she asks.

Gabriel at this point, nearly chokes on his beer!

'Is the nettle beer not to your liking?' I ask.

'It's more than just twisting yourself into knots,' I explain. 'It helps you free your mind, de-stress, truly relax. Your flexibility will improve with practice.'

'We manage all right as we are!' Gabriel adds. 'Don't we babe?'

'Can you show me something easy?' Eleanor asks.

'Right, well first of all, you have to concentrate on your breathing,' I begin. 'Inhale through your nose and exhale through your mouth. Something you can try is just a single exhalation to relax the skin on your face when under stress; or you could simply close your eyes for a moment of quiet reflection between phone calls at work. Once you start it'll soon become a habit,' I explain.

'Don't go listening to all that crap El,' Gabriel quips.

'Right,' I continue, ignoring him. 'Try this,' I say. 'Start on all fours,' I begin, knowing already we've got an audience, 'inhale as you lift your tailbone and head, and make your back concave.'

'What does that mean?' Eleanor asks.

'Dipped,' I explain.

'I know that! I remember learning it in maths at school. Is my tailbone my bottom?' she asks.

'Just above,' I remind her.

'Keep your elbows straight, and look up at the ceiling, keeping the back of your neck soft,' I explain.

'That's my favourite place!' Gabriel informs us.

'As you exhale, round your back. Let your shoulder blades spread wide apart to release the tight muscles in your upper back and neck,' I continue.

'So, what's this called?' Gabriel says, trying to distract us.

'The cat pose,' I explain. I continue talking Eleanor through the exercise, explaining it will develop her concentration and awareness.

'She can't very well do that in the surgery,' Gabriel comments.

Or home, come to think of it!

'Come on you two, it's your turn,' I say, inviting them to give some awkward positions a go. Which of course is hilarious fun, ending with us all collapsing on the floor in each other's arms. If yoga hadn't worked, then laughter would have surely lightened our souls.

We drag ourselves back to the comfort of the sofas, Jim nudging me, indicating the contents of the shelf under the coffee table, where on top of the weekend papers and beside the basket of remote controls, lies a guide of 'Images you should not masturbate to'!

'We're going away in September,' Eleanor begins. 'Why don't you join us?' she suggests.

'Where are you going?' I ask.

'My parents have a chalet in a little village in Austria,' she tells us. 'They hardly ever use it now. We used to go skiing as children, but it's just as beautiful in summer,' she explains.

'What do you think?' I ask, turning to Jim.

'Sounds fun,' he agrees.

'It'll be a blast!' Gabriel says.

'That's settled then, you'll be our guests, let me show you some pictures,' Eleanor says, squashing next to me on the sofa. 'You do like walking, I hope?'

'Yes, but I'll have to start brushing up on my language skills,' I say, trying to think of a phrase.

'Perfekt!' Eleanor says.

'I didn't know you could speak German,' I say, catching Jim's expression, which looks as astounded as mine.

'There's probably a lot you still don't know about me yet,' she says. 'I'm sure that'll all change in September though.'

We continued chatting and drinking for some time before I realised what time it was.

'Shall I start preparing the dessert?' I ask.

'What, before we've eaten?' Gabriel laughs.

'So, what's on the menu?' Jim asks.

'El love, just grab the menu off the board would you,' he asks.

This time it was Jim who nearly spat his beer out! It appeared we were having a takeaway. But delivered of course!

'El, come and help me in the kitchen,' I ask.

'Oh, OK,' she agrees, a little reluctantly. 'I was rather hoping you'd do that.'

'You have got individual glass dishes?' I ask, realising I should have perhaps brought some with me.

'Yes,' she says, opening the cupboard doors to reveal a selection of beautiful glass and chinaware.

'These are perfect!' I say, astonished, realising we'd at least have something to eat from!

'They're not mine!' she admits, denying all ownership. 'They were here when I moved in.'

'They're beautiful Eleanor,' I explain.

'I've never really noticed,' she admits.

On closer inspection, I noticed there were six of everything, even the mugs in the cupboard above the kettle all matched, something I believed were allowed to reflect your personality, often acquired as gifts from loved ones over the years. Just as long as the message wasn't too personal to grace the table! I even prefer certain ones, depending on the drink—a heavy one for coffee, and for a herbal tea, it just has to be my large, white fluted mug, with a heart design on the front. Frank's had been a mug he'd brought with him, a gift from Grace one Father's Day. Gabriel's wife, I realised, must have been a meticulous woman and quite the domestic goddess, unless of course she'd inherited it all herself. It would explain why it was still sat in the cupboards.

Appearances, I realise, can be very deceptive, recalling looking out at the washing hung on the line next door, when Frank and I had just moved in. Along with Megan's baby clothes, there had been a rather large pair of ladies' briefs and an exceedingly large bra, not one designed for a lactating mother, but leading me to believe her mother was rather a large lady; were in actual fact, Lucy was very petite and flat chested! It transpired, her sister had been staying with her!

'Right,' I begin. 'The first thing we need to do is poach the blueberries.'

'You mean we've got to go and find 'em!' Gabriel exclaims. To which I begin wondering if agreeing to going away together, was such a good idea after all!

'Add a little limoncello,' I continue, addressing Eleanor and ignoring Gabriel.

'Now you're talking!' Eleanor says, sounding more enthusiastic.

'Right they only take a minute,' I say, taking them off the heat to cool.

'While they're cooling, pour the cream into this bowl,' I continue, allowing her to prepare the dessert without even realising; something no one has obviously taught her before. 'Now add six tablespoons of limoncello,' I instruct her.

'Sounds like Nigella,' Gabriel interrupts again. 'All we need now is Barry White playing in the background!'

'Which is a tablespoon?' she asks.

'The largest one,' I tell her, finding one nestled underneath the dessert spoons.

'Once you've done that, add six tablespoons of this,' I say, passing her the dessert wine.

'Now whisk it together, until it's floppy and just holding its shape,' I continue.

'Too much alcohol can have that effect on me!' Gabriel informs us.

'Gabriel, I'm trying to concentrate here, if you don't mind,' Eleanor pleads.

'Right put a few blueberries in the bottom of each glass,' I ask. 'Then scatter over some of the Amaretti biscuits, then the syllabub.'

'The cream mixture?' Eleanor asks.

'Precisely!' I answer.

'So exactly how much?' Eleanor asks.

'Oh, just a dollop,' I tell her. 'I didn't mean that precise!' I say, realising we were on a completely different wave length to each other.

'Now, just continue layering twice more, ending with syllabub and topping with a few blueberries and Amaretti biscuits,' I tell her. 'It's a bit like constructing a lasagne.' Regretting it, almost as soon as I'd said it!

'Right, they can go in the fridge to chill,' I say, helping Eleanor carry them over.

'Shall I help you set the table?' I offer, before realising it had obviously been a while since it had seen food. There was an accumulation of everything other than what you'd expect to find there, from mail and magazines, to Gabriel's clean overalls.

'That'd be a nice change,' Eleanor admits.

When the food had arrived, it hardly mattered there were no candles or cruet set, the food being very well received, it was now nine o'clock, and probably far too late to be sitting down to dinner. Nevertheless, despite having already eaten enough, we all tucked into our desserts.

'Wow, this is delicious El, did you make it?' Gabriel asks, tucking into his syllabub.

'Under the watchful eye of Molly,' she admits, accepting some of the credit. 'And they're our very own glasses. I found them in one of the cupboards.'

'I thought they looked familiar!' Gabriel says. 'I don't think we need to worry about eating whilst we're away,' he concludes, Jim casting me a glance!

'I can give you lessons,' I tell Eleanor. I catch Gabriel about to say something, but instead takes another mouthful of dessert.

'I'm stuffed!' Gabriel declares.

Well I suppose that's compliment enough, I think to myself.

'You normally only get a wet cloth and after dinner mint if you eat in!' Gabriel informs us.

'Delicious,' Jim compliments, as he finishes his own. 'Thank you, girls.'

'That reminds me, I brought some chocolate liquors,' I say, remembering where I'd left them, reminding Eleanor it seems, to bring out the schnapps.

'A quaint Austrian tradition!' she informs us.

A couple of hours later, our taxi arrives, and we bid farewell to our hosts.

'Thank you both for a lovely day,' I say, realising just how long we had actually been there. 'Don't forget to practice what I taught you,' I tell Eleanor.

'My thoughts exactly!' Gabriel quips.

'Right, we'll leave you to it!' Jim adds.

'What're they like!' I say to Jim, as we leave together.

'They're just in love,' he reminds me.

'Aren't we?' I ask.

'Yes, but they're younger, well, El is,' he says.

I consider for a moment, before responding, 'I wouldn't change a thing!'

Chapter 27
Friends and Lovers

Jim informed me he'd got a few errands to run, but would be back for lunch, having unbeknown to me, already arranged to see Angela, although not quite as she had imagined.

'Hello James!' Angela greets him at the door. 'Did you miss me?'

'Did you have a good holiday?' he asks.

'Wonderful!' she admits.

'Angela, I need to talk to you,' he says, avoiding her advances.

'Why don't I like the sound of this,' she says, sitting down.

'I'm sorry Angela, it was fun while it lasted.'

'Why, because I went away with my husband?'

'No, because I've seen the error of my ways,' he admits.

'You sound like you've swallowed the New Testament!' she continues. 'You're not applying to fill the shoes of Saint James, are you?'

'No, I love Molly,' Jim says. 'You're a fabulous woman, but it could never work between us, we're too different.'

'They say opposites attract,' Angela interjects.

'I can't really see you down on the farm in a pair of wellies,' Jim says. 'You belong here, with all the things I can't give you.'

'You gave me so much more,' Angela admits.

'I'm sorry Angela, it was fun though, wasn't it?' he reiterates, recalling their liaisons.

'Short but sweet,' she replies.

'So, no hard feelings?' he asks, relieved.

'Apparently not, anymore!' she says, smirking.

Then we'll say no more about it,' Jim concludes.

'My lips are sealed,' Angela tells him. 'But you know where I am if you change your mind.'

Jim leaves, without looking back, and with no intention of ever returning as he drives away towards Molly.

'Guten Abend!' I greet him on his return. 'You weren't long.'

'No, it didn't take as long as I expected,' he says.

'Are you all right Jim?' I ask.

'Yes, why?'

'Oh nichts,' I reply.

'Sorry, what did you say?' Jim asks, still a million miles away.

'Come here,' I say, wrapping my arms around him and giving him a kiss. 'Go and relax in the garden whilst I make lunch.'

'Thanks, I might just do that,' he says. 'I do love you Molly.'

As summer came to a close, a new life was beginning in the shape of Aidan James, born to Kate and Sam, a little earlier than expected, on the thirty-first day of August at eight o'clock in the morning. The announcement arrived via text message, courtesy of Kate's mother Angela, along with some other unexpected news.

'Jim, there's a message from Angela on your phone,' I shout to him in the bathroom.

'I'm sorry Molly,' he pauses, returning to the bedroom. 'I had wanted to tell you.'

'Then, why didn't you?' I ask, puzzled.

'I didn't want to lose you,' he replies, coming to sit down beside me.

A nasty thought crossed my mind. He'd been expecting a text from Angela all along, but not with news of Kate's baby. That'd explain why he never lets his phone out of his sight!

'I'm actually glad you've found out. I can't keep it a secret any longer,' he admits.

'You'd better explain,' I tell him.

'I slept with Angela!' he says.

'When?' I ask, hardly believing what I was hearing.

'It's over now,' he says.

'When?' I repeat, now feeling quite sick.

'When you were away at Sophie's,' he informs me.

'How could you!' I cry.

'I wasn't thinking straight. I missed you. I thought I'd lost you and you weren't coming home.'

'It didn't take long for you to move on,' I say.

'It wasn't like that,' Jim stresses.

'Well, what was it like?' I ask, regretting it as soon as I'd said it.

'It wasn't real,' he says, trying to explain himself.

'What do you mean?'

'It was just an escape I suppose. Like getting drunk,' he explains.

'You're still responsible for your actions,' I tell him.

'I'm sorry,' Jim pleads.

'Did it happen more than once?' I ask.

'Yes, several times,' he admits.

'So, were you drunk when you decided to see her again?' I ask.

'No,' he says quietly.

'There's no need to let it spoil what we've got, or upset anyone else,' Jim says.

'You mean, don't spoil things for Angela, don't let her husband find out. And what about your daughter, poor Sarah, and your late wife,' I ask, still unable to fully comprehend what I'm hearing.

'I know, I was foolish,' Jim admits. 'If only you hadn't left.'

'But it was your idea,' I shout. 'You encouraged me,' I remind him.

'It was done with my best intentions,' he declares.

'So you could explore other opportunities! I suppose she'd be there if I was to leave again,' I say.

'I would never let it happen again. I would never let you leave me again. I was a fool Molly,' he says. 'Trust me, I love you.'

'Just go Jim,' I order, opening the door, 'and take your phone with you.'

'Please consider what I said,' he says, as he leaves.

Jim continued phoning throughout the day, and I continually ignored him, leaving my phone upstairs while I sat downstairs considering everything that had happened, little things coming back to me: James's sermon about adultery, wondering if he could have possibly known, then I remembered Angela addressing Jim as James. I was so angry and upset, all I could do was cry.

The following morning after a very disturbed sleep, I unsuspectingly opened the door to Jim. Not wanting to cause a scene I allowed him in.

'Have you had time to think?' he asks.

'I've done nothing but think,' I tell him.

'I couldn't sleep, so I waited till I'd milked the cows before disturbing you,' he says. 'I am truly sorry Molly,' he continues, 'if we sort this out, we can still go to Austria.'

'You can forget going anywhere with me,' I quickly retort.

'So, shall I tell Gabriel we're not going?' he asks.

'You can tell him what you like,' I say, hardly caring about anyone else, or what they might think.

'So, you're not going?' he asks.

'Perhaps you should ask Angela,' I suggest.

'I don't want to go with her,' he tells me.

'Well don't go away! I'm sorry Jim, I can't cope with holiday plans right now, or you, come to think of it!' I tell him, showing him the door.

Sarah was the next to visit, realising something was wrong. No doubt Jim having sent her, realising I wouldn't say anything to her.

'I don't understand what's happened,' she asks, 'and Dad won't say.'

'I'm sorry Sarah, I'm afraid I can't tell you either.'

'Has Dad upset you?' she asks. 'I suppose that's a daft question, isn't it?'

'I'm afraid he's put me in a difficult position,' I say, choosing my words carefully.

'I'm sure you can work things out,' she says. 'I know he loves you. He's devastated.'

'Can I do anything for you?' she offers. 'I don't mind getting some shopping for you. I'll even talk to Dad if you want.'

'Leave it with me.' I eventually tell her.

'I'm worried about you Molly.' She says, genuinely concerned.

'I just need time to understand it myself,' I say.

'Please don't say it's got anything to do with that frightful woman?' she asks.

'Who?' I ask ignorantly.

'Kate's mother,' she reminds me.

'No, don't worry Sarah,' I say, hopefully allying any fears. Despite being angry, I wasn't prepared to hurt Sarah unnecessarily. Recent experience had taught me to think first, before saying something I might possibly regret.

'Well, I do have some good news,' she smiles. 'Kate gave birth to a beautiful little boy yesterday. I have an adorable nephew.'

'Have you seen them?' I ask.

'Yes, I went to the hospital last night. She's coming home later today,' she informs me. 'Look, I took some pictures,' she shows me, including one of Jim holding his new born grandson. My heart breaks just a little more, as I hold back my tears, realising I should have been with him to share the moment together.

'I hope mother and baby are both well?' I ask.

'They're both well. Sam said the birth was pretty straight forward, no complications,' she tells me, as if describing the birth of a calf!

'Was Kate's mother there?' I ask.

'No, she'd been earlier in the day. They like to restrict visitors,' she informs me.

'I'll go and see her in a few days,' I say, 'once she's got back home and settled.' Realising it'll be on my own.

'She'd like that,' Sarah says.

'Please don't let your dad or I spoil your happiness,' I say, realising it couldn't have happened at a worse time.

'Don't worry, I'm sure you'll work things out,' she says. 'You mustn't let my dad change anything between us. We love you Molly. Let me know if there is anything I can do, won't you?' she reiterates, before leaving me to consider what I am going to miss sharing with Jim.

Eleanor was next to call, just ten minutes after Sarah. Jim had obviously spoken to Gabriel, or quite possibly, both of them.

'You do realise Jim's in bits,' she begins, wrapping her arms around me. 'He didn't say what had happened, and I don't need to know, unless you want to tell me. He just said you wouldn't be coming away with us, that you'd had a falling out.'

'It's nothing to do with going away with you,' I assure her. 'It's just, I can't contemplate being in such close proximity to him right now,' I explain, close to tears again.

'What's he gone and done?' Eleanor asks, now even more concerned.

'Oh, it's complicated,' I explain.

'Men are, isn't that meant to be part of their appeal?' she says. 'Is there anything we can do?'

'No,' I say.

'You can confide in me,' she says. 'I am after all a medical receptionist.'

'Thank you Eleanor, I'll remember that.'

'You probably just need time to reflect, come to terms with things,' she advises, 'but don't go running away this time, talk to me.'

'Can I make you a cup of tea?' she asks. 'I can do coffee, if you'd prefer.'

'No, let me,' I say, smiling to myself, inviting Eleanor into the kitchen.

'You do have a lovely home,' she compliments, admiring my collection of photographs on her way through, glancing out of the window at the garden.

'I'm afraid we'll have to sit inside today,' I say, placing the pot of tea on the table, looking out at the rain, reflecting my sorrow.

'I think I've got a teapot somewhere,' she says. 'I just never think to use it.'

'Would you like a slice of cake?' I ask, realising it won't now get eaten.

'Oh, yes please!' she accepts. 'Obviously homemade!' she says, examining it.

'It's that obvious, is it?' I ask.

'Why, yes, you can't find anything this good online!' she informs me. 'Have you ever been to a little place called "Kate's Cakes"?' she asks. 'Her cakes are amazing! Especially the cupcakes, and you can even take them away!'

'I actually supply the cupcakes,' I explain. 'Kate is Jim's daughter-in-law.'

'Really! Well, that explains it. I told you, you could go into business. I now know who to ask if I ever want to host an afternoon tea party,' she says.

'It isn't difficult, I could show you some time,' I offer. 'You do have a lovely tea set to serve it on,' I remind her.

'I'll think about it!' she considers. 'We could have a little tea party, the four of us. Oh, sorry Molly, I wasn't thinking,' she apologises.

'It's all right,' I say. 'It'll take a bit of getting used to, I know.'

'Introduce me to all these people?' she asks, admiring all my photographs and changing the subject, as we carry our drinks through to the living room.

'Well this one is my favourite,' I say, handing her a framed photograph of Frank laughing. 'I took it myself,' I explain, remembering the occasion: his eighteenth birthday, he hadn't been looking, lost in the moment. I'd kept it hidden away at the time, along with my feelings for him.

'So, was this Jim, in his youth?' she asks.

'No, it's Frank,' I say, realising she'd never known him. 'He died, before I met Jim,' I explain.

'Oh, so he was your husband?' she asks.

'No,' I say, continuing to share our story.

'That's so sad,' she concludes. 'So do they all have such wonderful stories attached to them?' she asks, casting her eyes over all the people I hold close.

'I suppose they do,' I consider, realising it would take more than an afternoon to absorb them all.

Gabriel and I are going out later for something to eat,' Eleanor says. 'Would you like to join us?'

'No, thank you. I don't think I'd be much company,' I say.

'Don't be daft, it might do you good,' she says, encouragingly.

'No, I think I'll have an early night. I haven't been sleeping too well,' I explain.

'Well, we'll have to have a girly day soon, while the men are busy, you can show me how to make those cupcakes,' she says, getting up to leave.

'Thanks Eleanor,' I say, genuinely appreciating her thoughtfulness. She had been right, there was more to her than I had first imagined. She could have quite easily ignored the situation, but instead took the time to visit me, she hadn't mentioned our holiday plans, they hadn't mattered, neither had her slip of the tongue. It's when these things happen, that you realise just who your friends really are.

Sarah continued trying her best to get Jim and I back together, or at least talking, inviting me round so Jim and I could talk on neutral territory, assuring me she would take the children out and not listen behind closed doors, or from the top of the stairs, as parents have been known to do! Then she'd asked if I could help to look after the children. Apparently, Jim had been meant to be looking after them whilst she and Henry went out, but had phoned to say he was going to be delayed, asking if I'd mind helping until he was able to get there.

'Tell your dad he doesn't need to bother, I don't mind staying. What time will you be back?' I ask.

'Oh, possibly eleven,' Sarah says. 'You can stay over if you like.'

'OK, I'll see you later,' I tell her excitedly, having not seen the children for a little while.

It appeared Jim had, after all, managed to arrive in time for Sarah and Henry to leave as arranged, it also appeared that Sarah had managed to set us both up, Jim as surprised to see me as I was him.

'I had no idea you were coming,' Jim says, innocently.

'You're forgiven,' I tell him.

'Really!' he says.

'For being here,' I add, 'that's all.'

'Oh, I thought you meant for what I did,' he says. 'You do realise we could be away now.'

'Yes, but that isn't the issue, is it?' I remind him. 'Are you still communicating?' I ask.

'No, look at my phone if you don't believe me,' he says, offering it to me.

'There's no need,' I say, 'I believe you.' I'd spent a lot of time thinking things through, regretting the way I'd treated Jim after he'd taken me to Sophie's to recuperate, without a thought for how he had been feeling, and something Sarah had said, about how we all struggle sometimes to make sense of things. We'd both made mistakes, we are only human after all, and that dreadful woman had just been waiting for an opportunity to seduce him.

'Does that mean I'm forgiven?' he asks.

'Well we can't go on like this,' I admit.

'Can we put it all behind us now, and move on?' he asks.

'I'd like that,' I agree.

'Good, because there's something I'd like to ask you,' he says, putting his arms around me.

'What, if I'll go to Austria?'

'No,' he says, holding me in his arms, and looking into my eyes, 'will you marry me?'

'Marry you!' I repeat, surprised.

'You're being a little presumptuous, aren't you?' I say, walking away to look across the fields.

'I love you Molly,' Jim continues. 'I want to spend the rest of my life with you. Say something Molly.'

'I'm sorry, I wasn't expecting that,' I tell him, not knowing what else to say.

'Will you at least think about it?' he asks.

'I'll struggle not to!' I admit.

Chapter 28
The Morning After the Night Before

Sarah was surprised, but happy to see both Jim and I appear in the kitchen the following morning.

'Did you forget you'd already asked Molly to stay?' Jim muses.

'I take it this means you've patched things up,' Sarah says. 'I'm so pleased, you belong together.'

'That's just what I said, isn't it?' Jim says looking at me.

'I was going to take Luke and Lizzie to see their new cousin later. Have you any plans?' Sarah asks.

'To spend the rest of our lives together,' Jim tells her.

'We're going looking at rings,' I tell her.

'Really!' she says. 'That's wonderful! Congratulations!' she continues, hugging and kissing us both.

'Mummy, why are you shouting?' Luke shouts from the other room. 'I can't hear my programme.'

'Grandma and Grandad are getting married!' she says, swinging Lizzie in her arms, who'd come to join in the celebrations.

'Can I be bridesmaid?' Lizzie asks.

'Of course you can,' Jim assures her.

'I haven't actually met Aidan yet,' I admit. 'I'd love to meet him,' I say. 'Shall we go and tell them our good news?' I ask Jim.

'There's no time like the present,' he decides. 'Just as soon as we've eaten breakfast.'

Angela's car doesn't deter us, as we arrive outside together. After all, it's Jim's home as well.

'It's fine!' I say to Jim who looks at me. 'It's over, we have to move on for the sake of Sam and Kate.'

'I love you,' Jim says, kissing my cheek.

'I know that. Don't worry,' I reassure him.

We let ourselves in and head towards their living room and the sound of a hungry baby.

'Hello James!' Angela greets Jim. 'This is a nice surprise! Oh, I see you've brought your friend.'

'She's actually my fiancée!' Jim announces.

'Congratulations!' Kate and Sam shout in unison, Sam shaking his father's hand and Kate taking me in her arms and kissing me. 'That's wonderful news!'

'We'd like to ask you something too,' Kate says. 'Would you be Aidan's godmother?'

'Thank you, I'd be honoured,' I say. 'Though I haven't even met him yet!'

'Mum, let Molly have a hold,' Kate asks her mother.

'No, don't disturb him,' I say, 'he looks settled.' Realising there'll be plenty of other opportunities. 'He's adorable,' I comment, peering over Angela's shoulder. 'What made you decide on his name?' I ask.

'Well,' Kate begins, 'we couldn't agree on a name, we'd considered so many. Then I realised he was born on Saint Aidan's Feast day.'

'So, what if he'd been born a day earlier?' Jim asks, leaving the room with his son.

'No, there's more to it than that,' Kate continues. 'Aidan, is the patron saint of Lindisfarne, and that's where Sam proposed to me,' she explains.

'Oh, that's a lovely story,' I say. 'How special!'

'You never told me that,' Angela says.

'You never asked,' Kate replied.

'We've decided James for his second name,' she tells us. 'We hadn't really considered it, until I noticed my mum using it.'

At which point, I look directly across the room at Angela. I wasn't going to let her threaten what Jim and I had together.

'I think I'll be going,' Angela says, handing Aidan back to Kate.

'Molly, will you have him while I see my mother out?' Kate asks, handing me her son wrapped up in a blanket.

'With pleasure,' I say, receiving him in my arms.

'Say goodbye to Jim on your way out,' I tell Angela, once Kate has left the room.

'How soon can you pack?' Jim asks.

'Why, we're not eloping are we? I'd quite like to get used to the idea first,' I say, considering I'd never been engaged before.

'I thought we could catch up with Gabriel and Eleanor after all,' he says.

Chapter 29
Anywhere with You

'We were just talking about you,' Eleanor says, opening the door to Jim and me.

'Bugger that! What the hell are you doing here?' Gabriel asks.

'You're engaged!' Eleanor says, noticing my ring, a rather large ruby. I had once dreamt of choosing my own ring, but then again, it would always have been a ruby, a symbol of romance and devotion. Jim's mother, it seemed, had obviously shared my taste, and remarkably the same slender fingers, even Jim's grandmother, as the ring had once belonged to her, making it even more special. I would of course have to choose my own wedding ring, as Kate was now wearing that.

'You've come all this way to tell us that?' Gabriel muses.

'And, to ask if you'll be my best man?' Jim asks.

'Well in that case, come inside!' Gabriel says, opening the door to let us in.

'Get the Champagne out of the fridge,' Eleanor demands.

'Were you expecting us?' Jim asks.

'No, why?' Eleanor asks.

'Just something you said!' Jim replies, accepting his glass of bubbling Champagne.

'To Jim and Molly, may you have a long and happy marriage,' Eleanor toasts, raising her glass.

'Thank you,' I say, after taking a sip, 'I hope you don't mind us gate crashing like this?'

'No, it's the best surprise ever,' Eleanor admits. 'So, have you set a date?'

'We only decided this morning,' I explain. 'I haven't quite got used to the idea myself yet.'

'Take as long as you like,' Jim says, 'just as long as we're together.'